QUARTZ CREE

SHY GIRL
& SHY GUY

QUARTZ CREEK RANCH

SHY GIRL & SHY GUY

**Kiersi Burkhart and
Amber J. Keyser**

darby creek
MINNEAPOLIS

Darby Creek
A division of Lerner Publishing Group, Inc.
241 First Avenue North
Minneapolis, MN 55401 USA

For reading levels and more information, look up this title at www.lernerbooks.com.

The images in this book are used with the permission of: © iStockphoto.com/Piotr Krześlak (wood background).

Front cover: © Barbara O'Brien Photography.
Back cover: © iStockphoto.com/ImagineGolf

Main body text set in Bembo Std regular 12.5/17.
Typeface provided by Monotype Typography.

Library of Congress Cataloging-in-Publication Data

Names: Burkhart, Kiersi, author. | Keyser, Amber, author.
Title: Shy Girl & Shy Guy / by Kiersi Burkhart & Amber J. Keyser.
Other titles: Shy Girl and Shy Guy
Description: Minneapolis : Darby Creek, [2017] | Series: Quartz Creek Ranch |
    Summary: "The beautiful gray gelding Shy Guy is just as afraid of people as Hanna
    is of horses, but when a greedy local couple steal him, only Hanna and her friend
    can get him back"— Provided by publisher.
Identifiers: LCCN 2015034005| ISBN 9781467792530 (lb : alk. paper) |
    ISBN 9781467795685 (pb : alk. paper) | ISBN 9781467795692 (eb pdf)
Subjects: | CYAC: Human-animal relationships—Fiction. | Horses—Fiction. |
    Bashfulness—Fiction.
Classification: LCC PZ7.1.B88 Sh 2017 | DDC [Fic]—dc23

LC record available at https://lccn.loc.gov/2015034005

Manufactured in the United States of America
1-38281-20006-8/1/2016

For Mom and Dad: thank you for taking a chance on me, and for all the sacrifices you made so I could ride horses.

—**K.B.**

For my amazing cousins, Timshel and Theodora: you were the heart of my childhood and I am so grateful.

—**A.K.**

CHAPTER ONE

Hanna pressed her cheek to the cool window as the clunky old Econoline van trundled off the highway. Hills carpeted in evergreens and wildflower meadows gave way to a cute, old-fashioned mountain town. It looked like it had been pulled right out of a painting hanging in her grandma's house, one of those perfectly picturesque country villages. A quaint diner sat between a candy store and a rock shop. Couples walked hand in hand down Main Street. And every store had a horse painted on the sign.

Horses. It was always horses.

At least Quartz Creek Ranch was beautiful— or it had looked that way in the brochures Hanna's

1

mom showed her. *As part of the ranch experience,* the brochure had read, *youth will be paired up with a therapy horse and given thorough riding instruction.* Just the thought of the horses sent shivers prickling up and down Hanna's arms. She retied her long, sandy-blonde ponytail for the tenth time and pulled her long legs up to her chest on the seat.

"Everyone!" The brunette who had introduced herself as Madison back at the airport waved at them from the front of the van. "We're almost to the ranch. If you look out the window on the left side, you can see our very own Quartz Creek!" She was one of the two head trainers at the ranch. The other was driving—a black guy who'd been the one waiting at the airport for her with a sign reading *Hanna.* He'd introduced himself as "Fletch," spoke with a thick New York accent, and wore a big cowboy hat. Both trainers looked like they were in college.

The two girls sitting up in the middle seat shuffled over to the left side so they could look out the window, crowding the skinny kid who'd sat down there first. Hanna had claimed the far back seat, thinking that was the best way to avoid attention—and to get enough room for her long, gangly legs.

But that plan had backfired.

"What's her deal?" asked the Latina girl with bushy hair, glancing back over the seats at Hanna—and not appearing to care that anyone else could hear her. "She hasn't said a word since we left the airport."

The redhead with the upturned nose shrugged. "She's probably messed up." *As if everyone here wasn't messed up in some way*, thought Hanna. Parents didn't send their kids to Quartz Creek Ranch for fun. It was rehab for "struggling youth," as the brochure had put it. Without using the word *rehab*, of course.

But Hanna wasn't a "struggling youth." Okay, so she'd made some bad judgment calls. She certainly didn't deserve being banished like this. Six weeks in the dead heat of summer in the middle of nowhere, Colorado.

You've always liked horses, Hanna, her mom had said as she filled out Hanna's application for rehab camp—even attaching a pristine school photo in the top corner. *Horses! You should be happy.*

Learning to ride will be great for your posture.

They'll teach you discipline and manners. You could use some of those.

The van took a sharp right turn, and Hanna grabbed the ripped seat back for balance. At least there was one rule about this place she liked: parents couldn't call or write letters. Kids couldn't even bring phones or computers with them. Quartz Creek Ranch was a no-contact zone for a whole six weeks.

Like going to Antarctica.

"This is Bridlemile Road," said Madison, gesturing out the front window to the gravel road that ran between a row of trees and a glittering creek. "Named for Will Bridle's great-grandpa. Mr. Bridle's family has ranched on this land for generations." Fletch followed up with a few jolly honks of the van's horn. Hanna closed her eyes and leaned back in the seat.

Maybe this whole thing could be all right, she thought. Maybe her mother sending her off to this remote place could be cool, as long as she was left alone to enjoy its natural beauty.

By herself.

Alone.

Maybe the horses were optional.

Soon the van stopped, and Madison bounded off to open the gate for them. Through the windshield, Hanna could make out a sign erected above it: QUARTZ CREEK RANCH. The letters were smoky and blackened around the edges, like a cattle brand.

Once the van had passed through the gate, Madison closed it behind them and hopped back in. "You may think Disneyland is the most fun place on Earth," she said conspiratorially, "but it doesn't hold a candle to Quartz Creek."

The girls at the front rolled their eyes and laughed to each other.

As the van drove by, horses trotted up to the fence on the other side of the creek, snorting and swinging their heads. Hanna's chest tightened at the sight of them.

"Ooooh," said Frizzy-Hair Girl. "I hope I get to ride that pretty black one."

Right—they'd expect Hanna to ride here. The tightness in her chest dropped into her stomach. Those weren't six-inch-tall plastic critters with painted-on manes, like the hundreds of toy horses she'd amassed on her bedroom shelves as a little girl—the ones that had made her mom think the ranch was a good idea.

No. Out in the field stood real, living, breathing horses, a thousand pounds each and all of it hooves and muscle. Even if Hanna could get *on* a horse, she'd never be any good at riding. She'd end up thrown and trampled, and her mom's long list of ways Hanna hadn't lived up to her expectations would grow longer.

Soon the van pulled into a driveway and parked in a lot in front of a big ranch house. Hanna waited until she was the last one in the van before departing with her backpack. Fletch was waiting for her as she came out the sliding door.

"You okay?" he asked when he saw her face.

Of course she wasn't okay. She could be hanging out with her friends back home—swimming in the neighborhood pool, going camping with her dad, and getting ready for track season. Instead, she was stuck here for six weeks.

"Fine," Hanna said. "I'm fine."

Fletch tilted his head, his hat almost slipping off his short hair.

"All right, well, head on inside the house, Hanna."

He said her name like he knew her, like they were friends already. It made her happy and sad, all at the same time, because she knew she'd disappoint him, as she always disappointed everyone else.

CHAPTER TWO

The ranch house had a towering, sloped roof that blocked the blazing sun as it set to the west. Madison led the five kids around the side of the house, past the main doors, and onto a screened back porch. She opened a smaller door there into the house. "First, the mudroom," she explained. "For your dirty shoes. Come on in."

Inside the house, the walls were painted rust red and it smelled like cinnamon buns. Hanna's mouth watered as she followed the others down the hall and into the main room, where a wood fire crackled invitingly.

"There they are!" An old woman with a wild

mane of curly hair shot up from her chair. "Welcome, welcome! Come on in. Dinner's almost ready."

"What are you cooking in there, Ma Etty?" asked Madison. "I smell cinnamon."

The old woman laughed. "Just wait. That's dessert." She ushered the kids inside, and Hanna took a seat on the end of the couch with Fletch and one of the boys from the van—the tall, dark-haired one who'd slept most of the trip.

"Hey," he said to her, holding out a hand. "I'm Josh."

Hanna was so surprised by Josh introducing himself first that she took a lot longer to reply than was probably normal.

"Hey," she managed to say. His blue eyes glittered as she accepted his firm handshake. "I'm Hanna."

"Cool."

"All right, all right," the older woman said, raising her voice a smidgen, but it was enough to get everyone's attention. "You'll all quickly find out we believe in action, not talk, around here—except this once. We're gonna talk a little, lay some ground rules. I'm Henrietta, but you can call me Etty."

"We all call her Ma Etty," said Fletch.

"You're welcome to call me that, if you like,"

Etty agreed. "I've worked this ranch for twenty years and raised three kids, so I've certainly earned a 'Ma' somewhere in there." Her smile was big and real, and unconsciously, Hanna unclenched her hands in her lap. "This here is my husband, Will Bridle."

A man emerged from nowhere, tall as a tree. His black hair was shot through with gray, and deep lines grooved his face. He reminded Hanna of an Indian chief dressed in settlers' clothing in some old photograph.

Mr. Bridle took off his hat, pressed it to his chest, and dipped his head politely. "Hey there. Name's Willard, but you can call me Will."

"We still call him Mr. Bridle," Madison stage-whispered to them.

"My overly polite horse trainers aside," said Mr. Bridle, raising an eyebrow at her, "I'm pleased to welcome you all to Quartz Creek Ranch." His voice was so deep it sounded like a bear growling. "I'm not going to lecture. You all know what you're doing here, as do Ma Etty and I. We picked each of you from our pool of applicants because we felt you'd make a good fit for our program and for each other. So our time together doesn't have to be punishment. Great things happen to people on this ranch—if they keep their minds open to it. Just be respectful. That's all I ask. Treat everyone and everything here with respect, and we'll all get along great."

Etty grinned widely. "And I welcome y'all too. Our home is your home. While you're here, don't hesitate to ask for help if anything is troubling you." She gestured to the two trainers, who stood up. "Madison and Fletch? Will you tell us a little bit about yourselves?"

Madison was the first to speak. "I'm Madison Clark. I just finished my freshman year at the University of Colorado, on a swimming scholarship." She jokingly flexed one arm. "On summer break, I come home, here, to the ranch." She looked pleased to say that word—*home*. "My only advice is to have fun. And steer clear of my horse, Snow White. I love her, but she can be a real brat."

Mr. Bridle nodded sagely. Madison plopped down on the couch, and Fletch went next.

"The name's Samuel Harris," he said, lifting his hat, "but everyone here calls me 'Fletch.' You know, after George Fletcher?" The kids all returned blank expressions. "Well, anyway. George was a famous bronc rider, like I hope to be someday."

"You will be," called out Madison.

"Thanks," said Fletch, dipping his head so his hat slipped over his sheepish grin, and he returned to his seat.

"At one time," said Ma Etty, "Fletch and Madison here were just like all of you. But I'll let them tell you their stories when they feel up to it. Know that you can trust them with anything—they've both seen a lot."

Hanna could tell that much from Fletch's eyes. Even when he smiled, they looked somehow sad.

"All right," Ma Etty went on, holding up a sheet of paper and scanning it. "It's time for you kids to introduce yourselves." She looked right at Hanna then, and a jolt of fear shot through her. Hanna sat up as straight as she could, as if her mother were right behind her saying, *Stop slouching all the time! Look at you, you look like a cavewoman.*

Ma Etty read the panic on her face and turned to someone else instead.

"Cade?" she asked the thin, pale, freckly boy sitting across the room. "Will you go first? Tell us a little bit about yourself."

Cade swallowed, and then a torrent of words tumbled out of him: "I'm Cade William Benison and I just flew in from California and you wouldn't

11

guess by how pale I am, right? Everyone says that, but it's because I really like video games and spend all my time inside or that's what my mom told me when she signed me up for this."

A long moment of silence passed. Then Ma Etty cleared her throat. "Wonderful. Thank you, Cade. The ranch is a fantastic place to rediscover nature and the outdoors." When Cade stayed standing, Ma Etty said, "You can sit. Who's next?"

No one raised a hand. Eventually she said, "How about you, Rae Ann?"

The redheaded girl with the upturned nose jumped at the sound of her name. "Oh, well, okay. Hi, everyone." She waved, as if the group was a pageant audience. "I'm Rae Ann Willis. Um, I'm from Vermont and my favorite color is blue and, um, I have a cat named Sadie. Who I miss. Already."

She quickly sat down.

"Thank you, Rae Ann. Who's ne—"

"I'll go." The short girl with the big, frizzy hair stood up, interrupting Ma Etty mid-sentence. "My name's Isabel, but you can call me Izzy. If I like you. Which I might not. But at least I'll be honest about it. I'm from Arizona, and I've always wanted to ride fast horses, which is why I'm here."

Hanna didn't think that was likely to be true. You didn't end up at Quartz Creek Ranch just because you wanted to ride horses.

"Thank you, Izzy," said Ma Etty.

"I'm not done," she replied, which made the old woman's face look, to Hanna, like a cat's when its tail gets stepped on. "Everyone should know I plan to be the best. The best cow milker, the best horse brusher, the best egg finder, the best—"

"Quite," interrupted Mr. Bridle. "Thank you, Izzy. Please take a seat."

Izzy's face turned bright red. Then she dropped back down to the couch with a loud *hmph*.

"Josh?" asked Ma Etty.

The quiet guy sitting next to Hanna shrugged and then stood up. "Name's Josh Chiu. I'm Chinese. Well, my dad's Chinese. But don't ask me to say anything in Chinese—I don't know it. I, uh . . . I live in Tennessee." He shrugged again and offered nothing else.

Ma Etty's hair looked even more frazzled than it had a few minutes ago. "Well, then," she said, taking a deep breath. "Thank you, Josh." He nodded and sat down.

Dread slithered up Hanna's spine. She knew what was coming.

"Hanna?" asked Ma Etty. "Can you tell us a little about yourself?"

Hanna crossed her arms over her lap but didn't move.

"Stand up," urged Fletch in a whisper, and Hanna felt her legs rising to the occasion without her permission. Every face in the room turned to her. She probably looked like a praying mantis, all long, gangly limbs, her hands uncomfortably crossed. And she was even taller than Ma Etty now that she was standing.

"Hanna?" the old lady asked her again.

"Um," sputtered Hanna. "My name's Hanna. Hanna Abbott. That's *A-B-B-O-T-T* . . . with two *T*s. And I, um, well, I grew up in . . . Michigan. And I . . ." She looked around the room, trying to think of anything else she could say, anything that wouldn't sound stupid and forced, but her mind was a blank, white sheet. She heard her mom saying, *Stand up straight! I can't believe I raised such a slouch. And that stuttering! You've never stuttered before, Hanna. Use complete sentences!*

"I like the color green and I steal."

She didn't mean for it to come out, but it was the most complete thought in her head—that nonsense responsible for this whole stupid trip to Quartz Creek in the first place. Hanna abruptly sat down and stared at the floor, unwilling to look at the faces around her after that impromptu confession.

The room was quiet for a second before Ma Etty said, in a low, sincere voice, "Thank you for that, Hanna. That was very brave of you. I'm sure everyone here has a thing or two they're not proud of, and it's important to remember our mistakes as well as our successes—so we can learn from them." Hanna's face burned like it were filled with lava. But Ma Etty clapped her hands together and moved on. "Well, I have one last thing to say before we sit down for dinner."

She paused for a long moment, surveying the five kids sitting around the room.

"Please know that no matter what, we're here for you. My husband and I started the Quartz Creek Ranch program as a place to learn and grow. We're all here to get better, and we can help each other do that. Do your best at each thing you do, and the rewards will return to you twofold. We give you free time on the ranch so you can pursue your own interests—please be responsible with the freedom you are given. When privileges are abused, they can be revoked. So if you have any concerns at all, any of us are more than happy to help, to care, or just to listen.

"Now let's get eating!"

\\\

After a huge dinner of roll-it-yourself burritos, Fletch and Madison led them back to the van for their luggage. Fletch took the boys, the three of them laughing over some inside joke they'd already come up with, leaving Hanna with Izzy and Rae Ann.

"Come on, girls," said Madison. "Grab your stuff and head that way." She pointed after the boys, where two little bunkhouses stood kitty-corner to the chicken coop and a huge, old barn with tractor parts piled up outside it like chopped wood.

They had to pick their way past chickens pecking in the yard to get to the girls' bunkhouse. "Honey!" Madison shouted up ahead, startling a hen. "Stay out from under foot or you'll end up McNuggets!"

The bunkhouse looked like something from an old western movie. The front porch creaked as Madison led them up the steps and through the equally squeaky front door. She pointed out the bathroom and then tapped a closed door. "This is my room. The rest is all you."

Two bunks occupied the main room, with a single bed relegated to the corner—enough to sleep five. Izzy and Rae Ann quickly took the bunk closest to the door and bounced up and down on the mattresses. Hanna wasn't about to sleep in a bunk alone, top or bottom, so she dragged her duffel bag to the opposite end of the bunkhouse and deposited it on the lonely bed.

"All the way over there, Hanna?" asked Madison, concern creeping into her voice. Hanna shrugged. "Okay, well . . . if the bunks are picked, we have a little tradition around here. Each new group gets to pick a name for the bunkhouse."

"A name?" asked Rae Ann. "Why? That's sort of stupid."

Madison hid a laugh. "I said the exact same thing when I was your age!"

"I still can't believe you came to Quartz Creek Ranch . . . you know, before," said Izzy.

Hanna couldn't imagine what someone like Madison had ever done wrong either.

"I know," said the horse trainer. "But let me tell you one thing: this place changes people. It changed me. And it will change you too. So as to commemorate the occasion and honor the tradition, we should give our bunk a name."

"Fine," said Izzy. "Like what?"

"Like . . . the Rockin' Ladies Cabin?" Madison suggested. "Get it? Like a rockin' horse?" Rae Ann let out a little snort. "Okay, maybe not."

Izzy raised an eyebrow. "It's not even a very good joke."

Madison pretended to look hurt. "Well, you come up with a better name, then."

"What about 'Pony Girls'?" said Rae Ann.

"But they aren't ponies," said Izzy. "They're horses. Ponies are small. Horses are not."

"Oh."

"No suggestions are bad," said Madison.

"Some are," said Izzy. "Like, 'Stinky Cabin' would be a bad name."

"Unless we were all sweaty and gross from being outside all day," said Rae Ann. "Then it might be a good name."

"Hanna?" asked Madison. "Do you have any ideas?"

Hanna shook her head.

"Cat got your tongue?" asked Izzy. Hanna said nothing.

"It's okay," said Madison.

"But how can we pick a name if she won't make any suggestions?" said Rae Ann.

"She can still vote."

So the brainstorming went on, until Rae Ann suggested Black Beauty's Cabin, because of the big black horse they'd seen galloping by in the pasture on the drive up, and everyone voted yes.

"All right," said Madison. "Time for bed. Go brush your teeth and get ready. Then it's time for lights-out."

Hanna waited until Rae Ann and Izzy were already inside the bathroom, giggling like hyenas, before she pulled her toiletries bag out of her duffel. Madison sat down on her bed beside it.

"Hey, Hanna," she said. "I know how you feel, you know. Us versus them? I've been through it too. I've felt like I'm the only one I've got. But do me a favor, please? Try and make friends. It's going to be a long six weeks if you don't even try."

"Okay," said Hanna automatically, but she knew it was going to be a long six weeks, no matter what she did or tried.

It was a horse ranch, after all.

CHAPTER THREE

The next morning was a flurry of activity. Madison told them to get dressed and get moving to breakfast, because they had a big day ahead. And breakfast went about the same as dinner the previous night: everyone else talked loudly, while Hanna sat quietly at the far end of the table.

Just the way she liked it.

Over scrambled eggs and bacon, Ma Etty addressed the kids.

"Who's ready to meet their horse?"

Cade threw up his hand and shouted, "Me!" Izzy laughed at him.

Ma Etty grinned at his enthusiasm. "Glad to hear

it, because we've picked out a special horse for each of you. You'll have a riding lesson with your horse every morning, under Fletch and Madison's instruction."

Every single morning? Hanna shrank lower into her chair, as if she could turn invisible and avoid her riding lesson altogether.

"Then, after lunch, we'll divide you up into pairs for other tasks the ranch needs done. And trust me when I say a ranch needs a lot!" She counted off on her fingers. "Weeding, mucking stalls, collecting eggs, feeding the chickens . . . We'll try to give you something different every day so you can have a go at lots of things, and you'll rotate partners as often as possible. After chores, you have free time until dinner."

"What do we do in free time?" asked Rae Ann.

Ma Etty grinned. "Whatever you want! Within reason, safety, and sight, of course."

After breakfast, the kids were led by a horse trainer out of the house, one at a time, until only Hanna was left, sitting alone at a graveyard of biscuits and eggs while Ma Etty and Mr. Bridle did dishes. Dread turned the food in her stomach to a roiling pulp.

"Hanna?"

At the sound of her name, Hanna glanced up. Madison smiled a wide, toothy smile and gestured for her to follow.

"Come on. It's time to go and meet your horse. The others are already out in the corral warming up."

This was the moment she'd known was coming since she got on the plane back in Michigan. A shiver slithered up her spine.

After clearing her place at the table, Hanna followed Madison's bouncing brown ponytail out into the warm summer morning. The ranch was alive in the sunlight, bright and green and bursting. As the two girls weaved among chickens pecking in the yard, Madison babbled about the horse she'd handpicked for Hanna. Gentle Lacey was a pony, she said—a little shorter than your average horse, standing at only thirteen hands high. A perfectly comfortable size for someone Hanna's age. Lacey was getting on in years but still knew how to run when Hanna was ready to run.

Hanna didn't have the heart to tell Madison she would never be ready to run.

They crossed a little bridge over the creek into a wide-open space clearly meant for horses. Closest to the bridge sat a small corral, with tall metal fencing;

behind it stood an old, weathered barn that was so big, it seemed to be peering down curiously over the rest of the ranch. An arena with a wood fence, big enough to pen in a whole cavalry, had been built to one side of the barn. In it, the other kids were already walking their horses around. Beyond the barn and the arena, a fenced-off pasture skirted the ranch and snaked off into the distance.

Madison led Hanna to the barn and opened the doors with a creak.

Inside, it smelled like old wood, leather, and manure—like horses. Hanna's hands were trembling in her pockets by the time Madison reached the stall on the far end of the barn and tapped the door.

"Here she is."

A brown nose reached over the top of the stall door, and Hanna took a step back. Madison patted the nose, crooning, "Hey, Lacey, pretty girl. How are you?" Lacey's furry head snorted and sniffled for treats, and Madison pulled a little brown biscuit from her pocket.

The pony's head was huge, even bigger than Hanna had expected—certainly large enough to bite off a hand. When Lacey's white teeth darted from her lips to eat up the treat, Hanna cried, "Watch out!"

Her yelp startled the horse and the trainer. "I'm fine, Hanna," said Madison, pressing a hand to her heart to slow it down. Lacey whickered on the other side of the stall door. "Come on over here and give Lacey a treat."

But Hanna was rooted to the spot. Lacey snuffled at Madison's arm again, looking for more treats.

"Hanna?" asked Madison. "Are you all right?"

Hanna tried to take a step forward, but she couldn't get any closer knowing the pony was there. Madison's smile faded.

"What's wrong?"

"I can't," Hanna said, and started backing away. "I can't."

"You can't what?"

Hanna swallowed. What could she possibly say? How could she tell a tough, cool girl like Madison she was plain afraid?

"I can't ride," said Hanna.

"What?" Madison frowned. "Of course you can. Not right now, of course, but that's why you're here—so we can teach you how to ride. As part of the program."

Hanna shook her head. "No, you don't understand. I can't ride. And I . . . I don't want to."

Madison's expression turned from confused to a little annoyed—the same expression Hanna's mom had whenever Hanna slouched at the dinner table or used the wrong past-tense version of *swim*.

"Well, now, that's a little different. But your parents said you love horses."

"Toy horses! When I was seven!" Hanna cried, exasperated. Those beautiful toys were all stuffed in a box in her closet now. "My mom forced me to come here, you know."

Madison's eyebrows went so high they disappeared under her brown bangs. "Forced you? That's not what she told me, Hanna. She said you've always wanted to ride horses."

"She's the one who wants me to want to ride," said Hanna. "But I don't. I don't even like horses."

Madison stood there, speechless. Then the barn door opened, and Fletch entered, leading a paint horse with Josh sitting on its back. He helped Josh off and said, "Find another helmet that'll fit you better in the tack room, and I'll tie her up over here."

"Fletch," said Madison. "I need your help."

Hanna's stomach dropped like a stone.

"What is it?"

Madison ran her hand over her forehead. "Hanna doesn't want to even get near little Lacey here. What do you think we should do?"

With a calm that reminded Hanna of old Mr. Bridle, Fletch stepped between them.

"All right. I've got it. Hanna, why don't you and I go outside and take a little breather, away from the horses? Madison, Josh's helmet is too small. Can you help out?"

"Sure." Madison turned and, without saying anything else to Hanna, trudged away. Hanna thought her face was probably purple with embarrassment. Madison must be furious with her.

"Hey, it's all right." Fletch's smile was broad and full of big, white teeth. She liked how genuine it was—and instantly felt guilty that she was going to disappoint him too. "Let's go talk outside."

Once they left the horse smell behind, Hanna could breathe better.

"There you go," said Fletch, reclining against the fence. On the other side, the kids walked their horses in figure-eight patterns around barrels in the arena. They were talking and laughing, already friends, already having a good time, already settled in with their horses.

"So, Hanna," said Fletch. "Can you tell me what you're thinking? Why don't you want to ride?"

She wanted to tell him—she really did. But how could Hanna admit she was terrified?

"Look," she said. "I really don't like horses, okay? I didn't want to come here. I even begged my mom not to send me."

Fletch studied her, and his gaze made her fidget. He looked right into her—and she could sense that he knew she wasn't telling the whole truth.

"I'm sorry you don't feel comfortable letting me in on what's really going on," he said. "But no one will force you to ride. We'll work up to it together. Why don't you watch the others for a while? When you're feeling less anxious, we can try again."

Hanna nodded. She didn't agree, but she didn't want to talk about it anymore either. Fletch patted her shoulder. "Don't worry so much, Hanna. There's no pressure. It'll work when it works." Then he turned and disappeared back into the barn.

Hanna felt even worse, having kept the truth from Fletch. So she did the only thing she could think of to do: she turned and jogged away, leaving the barn behind.

Running made sense when things got bad. When she ran, she could escape anything—including angry store owners who'd caught her stealing.

As her shoes hammered the dirt with a dull *thok, thok, thok,* Hanna felt the rush start at her throat and work its way down to her toes, calming her mind, letting her forget all about the barn and Lacey and Fletch and Madison, and about how she'd told her mom this place wouldn't work out.

Her mom hadn't listened. She never did.

Thok, thok, thok. Soon Hanna's thoughts were replaced completely by the steady beat of her feet.

They carried her away from the barn, away from the other kids talking and laughing in the corral. Her feet pounded the grass as she followed the fence line uphill. The air turned chilly as she ran through the shadow cast by a huge butte standing a hair east of the ranch. The butte was gently sloped and green on one side, then jagged and rocky on the other, like a giant had sliced off a chunk of it for buttering his toast.

After a while, Hanna's panic faded and she slowed down to a walk. Up ahead the pasture fence dipped abruptly. She stopped at the dip and gazed down, still breathing hard from her run.

She found herself standing at the top of a small crest. At the bottom of the slope, Quartz Creek bubbled along into a copse of nearby cottonwoods, the pasture fence trailing alongside it. The day was starting to heat up, and Hanna wished she could get closer to the creek, maybe dip her toes in it—but that would involve climbing over the fence and possibly coming face-to-face with a horse.

Besides, she'd have to climb over not one but two fences to get there. Another fence, constructed haphazardly with wood stakes and kinked wire, sectioned off a smaller pasture inside the larger one—and with it, a chunk of the creek.

What was this little pasture for? Were the Bridles keeping something separated from the other horses? Hanna didn't think she actually wanted to know.

Something moved in the trees. Hanna jolted. Whatever it was, it ambled around down by the creek, hidden by a low-hanging bough—and far enough away that Hanna could only hear the occasional rustle.

Then a white tail flicked.

A horse!

Hanna backed away from the fence. But the tail swished back and forth, as harmless and peaceful as a blade of grass blowing in a breeze. After a while the grazing horse turned around and emerged from the trees.

Hanna let out a loud gasp. It was beautiful—the prettiest horse she'd ever seen in real life, though from this distance, it looked like a toy. A white-flecked mane billowed down the powerful, faintly curved neck. Its coat was steel gray and shot through with white stars, like the horse had once been all white until someone dumped soot on it. Its barrel chest and sleek body reminded Hanna of a horse you'd see pulling a king's carriage in Victorian England.

Right then, it looked up—and spotted her. Hanna and the horse stared at each other, eyes locking across the pasture. Neither of them moved, each frozen in shock at the other's sudden appearance.

She should be afraid of it—what if the horse decided to come check her out?—but she found it impossible to look away.

Then the horse reared, flicked its silver mane

back, and galloped off into the trees.

Hanna stood there, awestruck, wondering if she had really seen what she thought she'd seen. Then she saw the horse's hooves had left holes in the grass. It had to be real.

What was that she'd seen in those wide, brown eyes? Fear? And . . . something else. Something dark, hidden, imperceptible.

Whatever it was, it made her chest ache. She felt like she'd seen a ghost.

"Hanna?"

She jumped at the sound of a girl's voice. It was Izzy, and her lips were twisted up with annoyance.

"What are you doing way out here?" Izzy said. "Everyone's been looking for you. Madison and Fletch told us you disappeared."

"I—I'm sorry." Hanna blushed purple again. "I didn't mean to."

"What do you mean you 'didn't mean to'?" Izzy crossed her arms and gave a huffy *pfft*. "How can you 'not mean' to run off?"

"It was an accident."

In the distance, voices called Hanna's name.

"She's over here!" shouted Izzy, waving her arms as people came down the road. "I found her!"

Madison ran up to Hanna, panting, looking both angry and worried. "Why did you run off like that?" Behind her, the other kids were whispering, until Fletch told them to keep quiet.

"I didn't mean to," said Hanna again. "I just started walking."

Madison let out a frustrated breath. "Well, I'm glad you're all right," she said. "So no big deal. But don't leave again without telling anyone where you're going, okay?"

"Okay," said Hanna. "I'm sorry."

Madison shrugged and shook her head. "Let's head back. It's lunchtime anyway."

Izzy rolled her eyes. "Great. I only got to ride for, like, five minutes."

"Come on," said Madison, giving Izzy a look. "Let's go help Ma Etty set the table. We'll discuss this later."

Izzy sighed and ran on ahead, joining the other kids in the front as they started walking back to the ranch.

Madison took up step next to Hanna like she was afraid Hanna might run off again. Hanna knew she should say something—apologize again for worrying her and Fletch, maybe—but all she could think about was the silver horse hiding in the trees.

So Hanna wasn't the only one on this ranch afraid of something. But what had made that beautiful horse so frightened?

CHAPTER FOUR

Before lunch could start, Ma Etty, Fletch, and Madison walked into the living room to talk, while Mr. Bridle got the kids seated at the table. Ma Etty's eyes occasionally flicked to Hanna. She knew by the sinking, nauseated feeling in her stomach that they were discussing her.

Would they send her home? That would be a relief, but her mother would be furious. *We spent all this money on that camp, and you couldn't even stick with it for one day?*

"So, Hanna, I'm just curious," Izzy said with a slight smile. "How do you 'accidentally' wander off?"

Rae Ann giggled.

"It's like, oops! How did I end up way out here?

Must have been an accident! Couldn't have been my feet or anything."

Cade reluctantly laughed too. Izzy was on a roll, and Hanna wanted to crawl under the table and die.

"I mean, seriously." Izzy's gaze pressed Hanna for a response. "Do your feet usually just do whatever they want?"

The laughter tapered off.

"Izzy," said Josh. "Leave it alone."

"What? I can't be curious?"

"He's right," said Cade. "Let it go."

"Jeez, guys." Izzy huffed. "Way to take all the fun out of everything."

Luckily, Ma Etty and the others returned just as lunch was served, and Izzy was forced to give up. Hanna tried to pretend that she hadn't even heard, but scarfing down green beans and tater tots at top speed didn't help calm her stomach. She wished she could be like that beautiful, frightened horse and gallop away into the trees.

\\\

In the afternoon, Madison handed out chores to everyone. Izzy and Cade helped Fletch move hay with Paul, the blond, mustachioed ranch manager, who reminded Hanna of Brad Pitt—if he were a cowboy from Colorado. Rae Ann fed and cared for the chickens with Ma Etty's help, and Hanna and Josh were put on garden duty.

Hanna let out a relieved breath to not be working with any of the animals after her disastrous morning with the horses. And an hour into mostly silent laboring on their knees in the dirt, Hanna decided she liked Josh. He was a fish out of water at the ranch, same as her; obviously from the city; and not a big talker. For a long while, the silence was comfortable.

"Fletch told me what that mountain's called," Josh said suddenly, nodding to the butte.

"Really?" said Hanna. "What is it?"

"Fool's Butte," he said. "I guess 'cause when prospectors started findin' quartz here, they thought they'd hit gold—they go together or somethin'. So they started up this whole town. Wasn't till they'd already dug up half the mountain that they realized there wasn't any gold at all."

"So that made them the 'fools'?" asked Hanna.

Josh shrugged. "Guess so."

She laughed. "I like your accent. Where are you from again?"

Hands black with dirt, he tossed a few more weed roots onto the pile. "Tennessee. Nashville. You?"

"Little place in Michigan called Sturgis." Hanna pulled out a weed, but only the leaves came off in her hand, leaving the rest of the stem stubbornly poking out of the ground. "Dang it. That keeps happening."

"You have to get it by the roots, and once you've got it, pull up slow-like." He showed her how to pinch the plant at its base and then tug out the entire thing, roots and all. Then he tossed the weed into the growing pile.

"You're good at this," said Hanna.

"Pull a lot of weeds in Nashville." Josh shrugged. "It's Mom's favorite thing to make me do when she grounds me."

"You get grounded a lot?"

"First four times she caught me smokin', I got grounded." Josh held up four fingers on one hand and then lifted the last one. "Fifth time, I got sent here."

Wow. Smoking? Josh couldn't be much older than Hanna, and she'd never even considered stealing a cigarette.

Hanna heard someone calling her name. She sat up and peered over Josh's head, and spotted Ma Etty waving at her from the edge of the garden.

Oh, no. She didn't know what Ma Etty wanted to say, but it couldn't be good. Hanna's spirits plummeted into the dirt.

"Hanna!" the old woman called again, shielding her eyes from the sun. "Can I speak with you? Josh, why don't you take a break inside and have some water. It's important to stay cool and hydrated when it's this hot."

Once Josh had gone inside, Ma Etty linked her arm with Hanna's, like they were old friends.

"Why don't we go for a walk?" she asked.

"Uh, sure," Hanna managed. Her mouth had suddenly dried up like a desert.

Leaving the garden behind them, Ma Etty led her out onto the gravel road that the van had come in on yesterday. She headed north, past the ranch house, toward the bunkhouses. Afternoon was in full swing and the sun beat down with all its June ferocity, making Hanna sweat even more.

Ma Etty adjusted her straw hat. "I heard what happened."

Tears burned their way from Hanna's throat, to her jaw, to the back of her eyes.

"I'm so sorry, Ma Etty. I told my mom not to send me here. I told her it was a bad idea, and she wouldn't listen. She wants me to be this great horse rider she can show off to her friends . . ." Then the tears broke through, despite Hanna's best efforts to keep them in, and filled her eyes so thoroughly the world became a blur. "I tried to tell her, Ma Etty. I did!"

Ma Etty didn't interrupt, but she turned Hanna to face her and settled a hand on her shoulder.

"I can't ride," Hanna managed between sobs. "I can't. Mom was wrong when she told you I love horses. She doesn't understand."

"Parents never do, do they?" Ma Etty's voice was so quiet, so soft and full of knowing, that it shocked Hanna into silence. "But that doesn't change that you're here now, Hanna. You're at this ranch, in my care, for a reason. And I see that reason right in front of me." Gently, Ma Etty reached out and tucked a stray lock of Hanna's long blonde hair behind her ear. Hanna couldn't look at her, too afraid of seeing disappointment on her face, too afraid of seeing pity there. But as the silence drew on, she finally did.

And Ma Etty was gazing at her with such kindness, such hope, and such . . . admiration? Hanna thought for a moment that maybe Ma Etty was looking at a mountain behind her.

"What's the reason?" asked Hanna, her voice trembling.

"I see such a kind, smart, sensitive girl here," said Ma Etty. "I see a girl with so much heart that sometimes, she's afraid. Sometimes things intimidate her." Her eyes crinkled when she smiled. It made her look years younger, not older. "That's not a bad thing. I don't think your mother intended to hurt you by sending you here, Hanna. I think she wanted something new and better for you. I think she wanted you to grow, and she knew you could do that here, with people who can listen and help."

"Except for Izzy," said Hanna with a sniffle.

Ma Etty gave a small chuckle. "Izzy's got a good heart. In fact, I think you two are more alike than you think." She took Hanna's arm again and resumed walking. They made their way toward the little path that bridged the creek. The musty old barn stretched up into the sky on the other side. "Hanna, what would you say to me giving you something else to do in place of riding lessons?"

It was so unexpected and so much more than Hanna could have hoped for, she couldn't respond at first.

"Yes!" she said. "Yes, please, oh please, yes."

Then she paused. "But . . . it's a riding camp. Can you do that?"

"Can I do that?" repeated Ma Etty. Then she broke out into a very un-old-lady-like giggle. "Of course. I can do whatever I want on my ranch. And if the idea of being near a horse is so frightening that it makes you run like a spooked horse yourself, well—I'm not in the business of forcing children to do things that bring them to tears."

Self-consciously Hanna wiped at her tear-streaked cheeks, but Ma Etty shook her head. "It's okay, Hanna. We all have our fears. Seeing a daddy longlegs has reduced me to tears more than once."

"Really? A spider?"

"Yep. Can't stand 'em. All those long, spindly legs and beady eyes and . . ." Ma Etty shuddered. "Having fears is part of being human. But we don't have to be slaves to them. We are capable of living relatively normal lives despite our fears. I mean, if I couldn't keep it together every time I saw a spider? Look where we are." She gestured at the huge old barn, the grass, and the trees. "Bugs everywhere! I'd be hopeless. So I had to learn how to manage my arachnophobia and work around it. I had to learn how to ask for help so I could get through the day."

"Who do you ask?"

"Mr. Bridle, of course. When I see a spider now, I call for him. He'll move the spider so I can get on with things. And knowing Will's there to back me up? It helps. Now I can even put a cup over the spider while I wait for him." She looked genuinely proud of this accomplishment and made Hanna feel less silly about the fear that had torn through her when she saw Lacey.

"But I don't know how to do that," said Hanna. "Who can I ask for help with a horse?"

"Growing up is about learning just that. I'll help you. Let me be your Mr. Bridle for now. I'm happy to rescue you when you're scared. Little by little, I'm sure we can find a way for you to be happy and healthy on this ranch. And we'll start by giving you jobs you can manage, okay?"

Hanna nodded almost imperceptibly.

"Tomorrow, when the others go to lessons, I'll show you some new things you can do. It'll be all right, Hanna." They turned around and headed back to the garden in silence. Josh stood drinking water by the pile of weeds.

"Remember," said Ma Etty, "dinner's in an hour."

Then she waved good-bye and went inside.

Hanna could feel that her eyes were red and puffy, but Josh didn't ask about them. Instead, he offered Hanna some water.

"Hydrate," he said and returned to weeding. As Hanna drank, she watched Ma Etty's strong back, trying to imagine how a little spider could make a woman like that cry.

CHAPTER FIVE

Izzy kept to herself that night in the girls' cabin, and Hanna was thankful. There was one thing Ma Etty had been wrong about: Hanna and Izzy were absolutely nothing alike.

In the morning, the other kids buzzed with excitement about their upcoming riding lesson. As Madison and Fletch herded them out of the dining room, Hanna stayed behind. Izzy cast her an indecipherable look as she slipped out the door.

Ma Etty appeared a few minutes later dressed in muddy overalls. "Ready for your new duties, Hanna?"

"As I'll ever be."

Hanna expected them to milk cows or maybe

feed the goats, but Ma Etty led her to the horse barn. Hanna's stomach performed a fabulous backflip.

Seeing her face, Ma Etty said, "Don't worry. I won't ask you to do anything you can't do."

Inside the barn, the scent of animal and leather made Hanna want to walk right back out again. She tried to visualize putting Lacey the horse under a cup, like a spider. It helped a little.

In the tack room, saddles of all sizes sat on racks, and halters and bridles dangled from hooks. Ma Etty opened a cupboard and pulled out a bottle of leather cleaner, a handful of rags, and a bucket.

"It's been a while since any of us had time to care for the tack," she said. "But good tack makes for safe horses and happy riders. Why don't you start with the saddles?"

Hanna nodded. Easy enough.

Ma Etty showed her how to pour cleaner on the rag and rub the saddle leather. Once Hanna got the idea, she took over.

This was a job she could do. A tremulous warmth seeped into her as Ma Etty left her to her work. The repetition of scrubbing made her think of running, of her feet pounding the ground as they carried her to safety.

Through the door, she could hear the horses eating and stomping, but it didn't frighten her.

\\\

That afternoon Madison took them to see the bees.

Everyone was excited except Rae Ann. She stood ramrod straight and refused to take another step toward the cloud of bees buzzing around the white bee boxes on the edge of the garden, even though the kids had all been outfitted in head-to-toe, bee-proof suits.

"They don't actually want to sting you," said Madison, who now waded into the swarm toward the first box. "And they won't unless you give them a reason to. They'll only sting when they're irritated."

Rae Ann adjusted her huge helmet and made an awful face.

"Won't they be irritated if you start stealing their honey?" said Izzy. She didn't appear to be afraid, though, and followed right behind Madison.

"That's what the gloves are for."

Hanna flexed her hands inside the thick gloves and picked up the empty cardboard box intended for hauling honeycomb. Collection was her assigned job, and after gulping air for good luck, Hanna waded after the others into the swarm.

The low hum of buzzing bees engulfed her. They landed all over her, tasting the suit's nylon fabric with their long, curled noses. No, not noses. Proboscises? Hanna remembered her sixth-grade science teacher calling them that.

"They're furry!" Cade cooed at one that had landed on his outstretched hand. "Like tiny hamsters."

"Tiny hamsters that will sting you!" cried Rae Ann, who still hadn't moved an inch.

"Cool," said Cade. "Let's keep one as a pet."

"A lot of people keep bees," said Madison as she opened the lid of the first bee box and set it aside.

"Who would put bees in their backyard?" asked Izzy. "Sounds dangerous."

"I'd rather have a cat!" called Rae Ann.

"Bees won't sting if you don't disturb them," said Madison. "Bees are pollinators. Without them, lots of plants don't reproduce. We wouldn't have fruits or vegetables without bees! Hanna, come over here with that empty box."

Hanna would have to venture deeper into the bee swarm, but with every inch of her covered in that dense, sting-resistant fabric, she was fine. She carried the box to Madison, who took frames full of dark orange honeycomb out of the beehives and began placing them inside it. If any bees were still clinging to it, she wiped them off, and they harmlessly buzzed away.

When the box of honeycomb was full and the beehive empty, Madison called for Josh. "The new frames, please!"

They did this for almost an hour, trading empty boxes for full ones as Madison made her way from beehive to beehive. There were six hives, and halfway through, Rae Ann suddenly spoke from her spot at the edge of the garden.

"You don't look stung," she said, surveying Hanna's suit.

Hanna smiled. "Nope. Not a single sting." Ma Etty was right. Everyone was afraid of something.

Rae Ann gazed out into the swarm. "I don't think my mom would like this," she said. Then she took a single, cautious step toward the buzzing swarm of bees. Inside her helmet her face was puckered and red, and she was biting her lower lip. After a step into the swarm, Rae Ann paused, as if waiting for something to happen. Nothing did.

Another step. Hanna offered her one thick, suited

arm, and Rae Ann seized it. A horde of bees on a mission to pollinate buzzed by, and Rae Ann let out a squeak, squeezing her eyes shut.

The bees passed, and when Rae Ann opened her eyes again, she was unharmed.

"Whoa," she said.

"Yeah, right?" Hanna picked up a box of empty frames. "Do you want to give these to Madison?" Rae Ann hesitated and then nodded. She let go of Hanna's arm and took the box. Expression resolute, she ventured into the humming cloud of bees like an explorer into an arctic storm. She stopped and paused a few times, shoulders shaking, but eventually made her way over to Madison.

In the mass of bees somewhere, Izzy yelled, "Glad you could make it to the party, Rae Ann!"

"My parents would never allow this," Rae Ann moaned.

Izzy barked a laugh. "Luckily, they aren't here!"

Hanna heard a squeaky voice in her ear. "I didn't see you during our riding lesson today." She turned to find Cade standing behind her.

"Yeah," Hanna said. "Ma Etty gave me, um, something else to do."

"Something besides riding? That's weird. I

thought everyone was supposed to ride. It's like our therapy."

Hanna forced out a laugh. "I guess I don't need therapy."

Cade frowned. "But isn't that why you're here? Because you stole stuff? Said so yourself."

Hanna swallowed. So far, none of the other kids had started this conversation. No one wanted to talk about what they'd done wrong, so nobody had asked. And she had preferred it that way.

"It's not a big deal," said Hanna evasively.

"Huh." Cade tilted his head. "Back in California, I beat a kid up."

What? This scrawny, freckled little guy couldn't be a fighter. He probably weighed half as much as Hanna, and she was pretty gangly herself.

"The horses are supposed to help me calm down," Cade went on. "'A healthy outlet' for my anger, or something."

"Is riding . . . helping?"

"No idea. But it's fun!" Cade shrugged. "So what are you doing instead of riding?"

"Polishing saddles."

"Hmm," he said. "Izzy was right."

Her name was like a paper cut. "What was

Izzy right about?" Hanna asked too quickly.

"That you're getting special treatment 'cause you're scared of horses." Cade tapped his chin. "Why are you here, then? I mean, it's a horse camp."

That familiar wave of hopelessness washed over her. "I've been asking myself the same thing."

"Maybe you could, like, get over your fear?" Cade said helpfully.

If only it could be that easy—as easy as walking into a cloud of bees.

CHAPTER SIX

Cade's question haunted Hanna over the next few days. *Maybe you could, like, get over your fear?*

Why couldn't she just "get over it"? What was holding her back? But even watching the other kids doing their riding lessons made her fear for them, as if the horses would suddenly stampede and they'd all get thrown off and trampled.

Over the weekend, the ranch schedule shifted, giving them more free time. But that meant more opportunities for Izzy to get on Hanna's case.

"Not coming on the trail ride today, Hanna?" Izzy asked as the other kids put on their helmets, their horses saddled and ready to go. They waited in front of the ranch house for Mr. Bridle to get his map and Fletch to check the riders' cinches for safety. At the front of the line, Madison rode her Appaloosa, Snow White, a mostly white horse with a mess of big, black spots on her rear.

"No," said Hanna. "I . . . I'm doing something else."

"Whatever," Izzy said, flipping some of her hair out of her face. "I'm sure going on a trail ride will be way more fun than anything you're doing here."

Behind her, Fletch's voice answered. "Actually, Hanna and I are working on a project together."

Great, thought Hanna. Now Izzy would really have some "special treatment" to hassle her about.

"Izzy," said Fletch, cocking his head, "your saddle's cinch is way too loose. Need me to show you how to tighten it properly again?"

"No!" Izzy led Fettucini a few steps away and checked the cinch herself. "I can do it."

Fletch raised his hands in mock surrender and went over to Hanna. "Hey. Are you ready?"

Hanna nodded. When Mr. Bridle arrived riding a muscular black beauty, Madison let out a little whoop. "Mount up, everyone!" she said. "It's time to go!"

Together, Hanna and Fletch stood out of the way as the trail riders got on their horses and strode off down the road.

Fletch closed his eyes and exhaled. "A few hours of peace. Whew."

Peace? Kind, quiet Fletch found her peaceful? She liked that.

"So what are we doing?" Hanna asked.

"You'll see. For now, go into the barn and grab two buckets. Fill one with water and the other with grain. Then go wait over in the small corral, next to the barn."

Hanna's heart skipped a beat. Those sounded like supplies for a horse.

"You want me to get what?" she asked in a small voice.

"It's all right, Hanna. I'm not going to ask you to do anything you can't do. Just meet me at the corral with those two things."

With that, Fletch tipped his hat and left.

Hanna did as she was told. Carrying the two buckets, she went to the corral and set them down. Then she waited.

Soon, on the other side of the pasture fence, Fletch appeared—leading the beautiful, silver horse she'd seen her first day on the ranch. Today he looked more like a horse in a movie than a figurine, with his snowy coat lightly dusted with speckles of ash, his silvery mane and tail flowing in the wind, and his powerful neck arched and taut.

He was beautiful.

But he didn't act at all like a horse in a movie. He stayed as far away from Fletch as he could, yanking against the lead rope with his huge head as the trainer urged him out of the pasture. The horse's ears lay flat against his skull and his nostrils flared.

When they reached the corral, where Hanna was standing, the horse stopped abruptly and pawed the ground. When Fletch tried to get near him, he backed away, ears flattening even more. His massive chest muscles bunched up underneath him like he might turn and bolt at any moment, and if Fletch didn't let go, he'd get dragged along behind.

This close to the horse, Hanna's blood rushed faster. He was the biggest, scariest animal she'd ever seen.

"Hanna," said Fletch, sounding strong and stern, "open the gate to the corral and put the grain inside. Make sure you shake the bucket."

"But . . . !" If she was inside the corral when the

horse came through, he might trample her.

"*Hanna.*" His voice left no room for objection. Shocked, Hanna grabbed the bucket of grain and went into the corral, shaking it as she went. The horse's ears tipped up and forward, and he stopped pawing. With Fletch moving out of the way, the horse edged toward the corral.

"Now put down the grain," said Fletch. "You're small enough—once he's about to go into the gate, I want you to slide out through the fence. Okay?"

Hanna's heart was pounding so hard she almost couldn't hear Fletch over the sound of it. She could get trapped inside the corral with a horse—a horse that appeared quite out of control, even with an experienced trainer.

Hanna set down the bucket, still shaking it to keep the horse's interest. The huge animal walked toward her, closer and closer to the corral's open gate.

At the threshold, he paused, and his ears perked forward. He was no longer looking at the grain on the ground but right at her.

Hanna froze, rooted to the spot, same as when they saw each other her first day at the ranch. His huge brown eyes stared through her, and she couldn't stop him. He took another step toward her, this time through the gate, and Fletch let the lead rope slide out of his hand.

"Hanna," whispered Fletch, "get out of the corral."

Her senses returning to her, Hanna squeezed out between the fence's metal bars. The horse, curious, walked after her into the corral—and Fletch closed the gate behind him.

When he realized what had happened, the horse turned, ears flat against his head again, and tried to go back out the way he'd come in. But the gate wouldn't budge. With deft fingers, Fletch reached over the gate and unhooked his lead rope.

The big, gray horse squealed, like a creature in a horror movie. Flinging his head from side to side, he pressed his entire weight against the closed gate. Hanna jumped back from the fence as the whole thing gave a metallic rattle. When he realized the gate wouldn't give, the horse turned and galloped back along the edge of the corral, knocking over the bucket of grain and scattering it across the dirt without a second look. Only one thing mattered to him: getting out.

Around and around the corral he went, ears pressed back against his skull, his huge nostrils flaring as he looked for a hole or weakness in the craftsmanship. Sometimes the horse would stop and turn and run back the other way, throwing his head over the top of the fence and taking huge, rumbling breaths.

Every time he completed a circle, he stopped on the other side of the fence from Hanna and stared at her. Fletch stood beside her, and they both watched in silence as the wild, terrible creature flung his head to and fro, mane tangling up in itself, and continued running in endless circles until he'd worked up a foamy, brownish sweat.

"What . . . what is he?" asked Hanna.

"He's hopeless," said Fletch. "Paul, the ranch manager, found him wandering around with the cattle up on the north end of the ranch. Abandoned, maybe, or escaped. Ma Etty wanted to find his owner and return him, because we thought for sure it was a mistake. By his head and conformation, we're pretty sure he's at least part Hanoverian—a kind of German sport horse—and we couldn't imagine anyone losing a fine creature like this and not desperately wanting it back. So we checked with the sheriff, but no one's reported a horse missing."

"He's so beautiful," said Hanna. "Why would someone intentionally abandon him?"

"I don't know," said Fletch. "After we started trying to work with him, though, we might not have returned him anyway, no matter who came forward. He was rail-thin when we found him, and he's obviously been abused. He had the saddle sores and was head shy to prove it."

"Head shy?"

"Don't raise a hand too close to his head," said Fletch. "He freaks out. It reminds him of being hit."

"So what did you do with him?"

"Nothing. Nobody could get him under a saddle without him biting or breaking loose. Madison, Paul, Ma Etty, and even Mr. Bridle tried—and Willard Bridle's the best horse trainer I know. He's worked with wild mustangs. But he had no luck, and no one around here has the time to start over from scratch with Shy Guy, what with camp going all summer."

"Shy Guy?"

"I gave him that nickname after he came to us, because he's so terrified of people." Fletch's voice dropped low, dangerously low, and his kind, almost sad face turned hard and cold. "Whoever owned him before really did a number on him."

Hanna glanced at the horse in the pen, still anxiously trotting in circles. Abandoned. Abused.

Afraid.

"Why did you put him in the corral?" asked Hanna.

"Shy Guy's back at square one, like he's never even been broken. No, worse—he's at square zero, because we can't even get close enough to trim his hooves. At least a green horse will let you do that." When Fletch leaned his weight against the corral fence, Shy Guy let out another terrible squeal and backed against the opposite fence. Fletch sighed and stepped away. "And if we can't trim his hooves," he said, "they'll grow out, break, chip, or even make him lame."

"I don't see what that has to do with the corral or me," said Hanna.

"Shy Guy needs to be socialized—just enough that we can trim his hooves, maybe get him into the barn again and off eating grass all the time, now that he's fattened up a little. Ma Etty hopes that if he spends enough time around people, in a safe, calm environment, we could work up to exercising him with a longe line. Even if no one can ever ride him again, he needs the attention and to not be alone all the time." He leveled his gaze on Hanna. "And that's where you come in."

"Me?"

"You. All I want you to do is feed him. Give him water and be near him. You don't have to touch him—you don't even have to get close. In fact, it might be better if you keep your distance. Just let Shy Guy get used to your presence. That's all I ask."

"But—"

Fletch held up a hand. "It's not the most glamorous job, but I think it will be good for both of you. And it's what Ma Etty wants. If you can't do it, you'll have to tell her yourself. You're the only one on the ranch with time to spare right now."

Hanna's whole body felt cold. Her job was to stay near that massive, powerful, unpredictable horse? He was way worse than little Lacey. He was wild. Out of control.

When she looked at him, Shy Guy stopped his pacing and looked back at her. His brown eyes roiled with fury. But under that, she saw something else— something familiar.

He was terrified.

Hanna knew exactly how he felt.

CHAPTER SEVEN

As morning turned into afternoon, the sun cooked Hanna like a fried egg on pavement. The high altitude made it worse—the sun never beat down this hot and bright back in Michigan.

Shy Guy had slugged down his water after all that running around and left the bucket bone-dry, so she'd have to fill it again. And she had to somehow get the empty bucket out of the corral—where a big, dangerous horse was currently tromping around.

Waiting until Shy Guy was distracted on the other side of the pen, Hanna edged closer to the corral fence. She snatched the bucket out from between the metal rails without him noticing. Whew. She wiped the sweat from her forehead and clutched the bucket to her chest.

First part completed.

Hanna had to use all her weight to push down the long, metal handle on the water faucet. As icy water shot out, she splashed some on her face and then finished filling the bucket.

When she got back to the corral, Shy Guy had stopped pacing and now leaned against the fence, looking as close to despondent as a horse could look. He shifted from one foot to the other and flicked an ear in her direction, but that was all.

Hanna set down the bucket. She'd have to get close enough to the corral again to slide it back under the fence, but she didn't want him to freak out and rear or kick when she got close. She walked around to the other side of the pen, hoping she could slip it under the fence without him seeing her, but as soon as she moved, he turned and followed her with his eyes. It was like a game of chicken—he wanted to keep an eye on her, and she didn't want to be seen.

So Hanna stood there, simply watching him, and Shy Guy watched her back.

Neither of them moved for a long time as she

thought about what to do. Shy Guy's tail lashed some flies that had landed on his rump, scattering them.

They were both baking in this heat. But he was a horse—he couldn't splash himself with cold water as she had. Hanna glanced down at the bucket of water.

He was calm, for now. But how long would that last?

Stuck between getting close enough to give him the water and keeping a safe distance, Hanna simply sat down and gave up her jeans to the dirt. Every time she moved, he flicked his ears at her, but the longer she sat still, the more he relaxed—and began to look bored.

And so, so hot. Hanna wasn't covered in hair like he was, but sweat still dripped down her face.

Finally, she stood up. Shy Guy glanced at her but didn't move. He looked more curious than anything.

She took a deep breath, picked up the water bucket, and edged toward him.

He focused on her, both ears flicked forward. Hanna took another step toward the fence. Dust rose from the edges of her boot.

Shy Guy's nostrils flared. He must be taking in the smell of her. Animals were sensitive to smell, she remembered. What if her human scent set him off?

What if it reminded him of all the humans who had done him wrong before?

Shy Guy readjusted his weight so he was standing on all four legs. Hanna could feel her pulse all the way up in her throat, in her hands, in her feet, pounding away like an out-of-control marching band. Water sloshed out of the bucket, surprising them both as it hit the ground.

Shy Guy retreated one step back, eyes wide, and stared at the wet spot in the dust as if it offended him. Hanna didn't move any closer, but she also couldn't look away.

He was majestic, no doubt about that. Majestic and terrifying.

And thirsty, she reminded herself.

Trying to steady her hands, Hanna took yet another step toward the corral fence. Shy Guy lifted one hoof, as if to match her step forward with one of his own back—but then set it down again. He focused on the water in her hands, his nostrils sucking in the smell.

One more step brought Hanna to the fence. Only a few rickety metal crossbars separated her from a thousand pounds of skittish muscle and hooves.

Panic welled up inside Hanna. Shy Guy's huge

head was so close she could smell him. He smelled like . . . horse. Sweat. Grass.

And he, undoubtedly, could smell her too. His neck arched and his sturdy, barrel-chested body poised to flee.

Hanna dreaded getting any closer, and she could tell Shy Guy was just as torn between his fear of her and his thirst. He wanted the water she had, but getting close—putting himself in a position where someone could hurt him—was too much for him.

She knew how he felt. When Hanna dropped something on the floor, slouched, or talked with food in her mouth, she'd panic like that. Had her mom seen? Would she be spending another evening balancing books on her head to "correct" her posture?

Hanna was always waiting for the other shoe to drop. After she'd started stashing under her bed the candy bars, energy drinks, trinkets, and even a pair of expensive sneakers she'd stolen, Hanna waited to be discovered. Her mom would blame Hanna's friends, her school, and everyone except herself—proving, yet again, how much she just didn't get it.

Shy Guy took a sudden step forward and Hanna jumped. He angled his head up and opened his mouth, exposing two rows of huge, square, white teeth. Hanna shrank back, almost dropping the bucket of water.

But he didn't lunge or snap with his jaws. He simply waved his lips around, open and closed, like a fish, in the silliest expression Hanna had ever seen a horse make. He reminded her of a frog prince trying to get a kiss.

A laugh burst out of her before she could stop it. Shy Guy leaned back, surprised by the sudden noise. Hanna covered her mouth.

"Sorry," she said to him. "Didn't mean to scare you."

Hanna was still holding the water, and again, Shy Guy waggled his lips at her. Well, if a horse was ever going to come right out and tell her he was thirsty, this was it.

Her fear dried up like that splash of water in the dust. She squatted down and pushed the full bucket under the fence. Shy Guy stepped back. His nostrils reached an impossible size and his eyeballs bulged, like he thought the water would bite him now that he'd finally gotten it.

The hard work was over. He had something to drink. But now Hanna's fear rose its massive head, and she realized how close she was to the fence—and the massive horse behind it.

Letting out a little wail, she skittered backward like a crab. Once she was a safe distance away, she let out a gasping breath and fell back in the dirt.

Shy Guy was startled too and stood uneasily a few feet from the fence. But the water drew him back, and with timid ballerina steps, he returned to it.

Hanna got up and dusted off her pants. The adrenaline finally caught up to her, and she drowned in a tidal wave of fear, happiness, and at the end of it . . .

Thrill.

She'd done it!

Shy Guy buried his muzzle in the bucket of water, scattering droplets everywhere. Hanna wrinkled her nose. She'd have to get him more water pretty quickly if he was going to be messy about it.

When he was done, Shy Guy looked up at her, ears perked—a thank-you, maybe? Hanna found herself nodding back to him.

It had never occurred to her how alike people and horses could be. Someone had hurt Shy Guy—and it had made its mark on him, the way hurt makes its mark on everyone.

Eventually, Hanna stood up. The horse watched her as she approached and put one hand on the railing.

He looked as if he might run; his entire attention was directed at her. But he didn't move.

"I'm sorry somebody did this to you," she said to him. His ears flicked back and forth, listening. "You didn't deserve it."

Something inside her—something alien and new and fearless—wanted to reach out and touch him. To comfort him. And to comfort herself.

\\\

That night they had a free hour before lights-out while Madison drove into town to swim some laps. Cooking in the Colorado heat all day had drained Hanna, and she wanted nothing more than to read in peace.

"I can't believe Hanna is getting another special new chore," groaned Izzy, falling back on her bed with a *thump.*

Hanna turned a page of her book and pretended to read.

"What's up with that white horse all covered in splotches, Hanna?" asked Rae Ann.

"He's not white," Hanna found herself saying. "He's gray. White horses have pink skin under their hair. Gray horses like Shy Guy have black skin. And he's not 'splotchy'—Shy Guy is a dapple gray."

Rae Ann tilted her head. "Shy Guy? That's a weird name."

"No, it's not," Hanna said. "Fletch gave it to him." She pressed her lips together. She shouldn't be telling these two any of this.

Izzy squinted at her. "He didn't have a name before?"

"No."

"Why not?"

"I don't know."

"Come on, Hanna. Tell us."

Hanna didn't say anything and tried to keep her eyes on the book.

"Fine," Izzy said. "I guess since you think you're so special, we should give you special treatment, right?"

Rae Ann giggled. "So-o-o-o special!"

"Hey, Rae Ann," said Izzy, turning away from Hanna, "know what would make her feel real special?"

Rae Ann opened her mouth but sensed she was walking into a trap and closed it.

"Putting some spiders in her bed!"

Spiders? Please.

Rae Ann's smile faded. "Madison will get mad at us," she said.

"Come on, goody-goody. Madison won't find out." Izzy waltzed to the cabin door. "I'm sure there are a few cobwebs hanging out here."

"Izzy, stop," said Rae Ann, following her. "I'm not going to put spiders in Hanna's bed."

"Why not? It's funny."

"It's mean. And if you do it . . ." Rae Ann's voice dropped. She sounded dangerous and very unlike herself. "I'm going to tell on you."

Izzy halted mid-step, and they stared at each other. Hanna regretted the mean things she'd thought about Rae Ann. She had it where it counted.

"Fine. Tell on me, *tattletale*," hissed Izzy. "You sound like a dumb little kid."

Without replying, Rae Ann stalked back into the cabin and climbed onto her bunk. Izzy stood at the door like she wasn't sure what to do anymore. Then she stomped outside and slammed the door behind her.

Rae Ann didn't look at Hanna, but under her breath she muttered to herself, in her most childish voice, "Meanie head."

After that, Hanna gave up trying to read. She fell asleep imagining Izzy stuffing spiders under her mattress, but she was glad it was her bed, and not Ma Etty's.

CHAPTER EIGHT

The next day, the need to steal something and get away with it consumed Hanna. She could slip a hoof pick into her pocket right under somebody's nose, or maybe swipe that pink halter she liked and stash it in her bag. Something to remember this place by.

But she'd feel bad stealing from the Bridles— and her mom would definitely find it once she got home. After discovering the goods under Hanna's bed, her mom had started performing weekly room searches. Anything that Hanna couldn't prove was hers was another tally on the "I'm So Disappointed in You" scorecard.

"Same thing again today," Fletch told Hanna as the other kids finished breakfast and went out to get started on their ride for the day.

Right. Shy Guy. Hanna's heart skipped a beat. No, it was a hop, a skip, almost a dance. She felt . . . excited to see him, not afraid.

Well, maybe a little afraid.

When she reached the corral, there he was, shining in the morning sun—its rays weaving through the fine silver threads of his mane.

Shy Guy's head shot up when she appeared. His whole body angled toward her, short ears standing straight up like a rabbit's.

"Good morning," Hanna said in a low voice as she approached the corral fence. Shy Guy tensed up, like he might put some space between them, so she stopped where she was.

They stood like that, looking at each other, in what was becoming their ritual.

Hanna checked his bucket. Still full. Good. In one corner, stray bits of alfalfa were mixed in with the dirt. Fletch or Madison must have fed him earlier.

Good.

Hanna flopped down on the ground. Shy Guy

shook his head and snorted, like he was displeased with the sudden movement, but he didn't move away.

After a while, he grew bored and wandered off, nibbling in the dirt for the leftover alfalfa. Was this it? Was this really her job, to sit here all day? All she could do was gaze out at the landscape—the green mountains with distant snowcaps, the blue skies—or she could stare at Shy Guy.

She did a lot of staring.

An hour later, Madison came and sat down next to Hanna. She was out of breath and dusty. Shy Guy cast Madison a suspicious look from the other side of the corral.

"How's it going over here?" she asked.

"Uh, I don't know, fine? Should something be . . . happening? I'm just sitting here."

"Good! No, that's great. How's he doing?"

Hanna shrugged. "Also fine, I guess."

"Perfect. Keep at it."

"I don't really get how this is helping."

"Ma Etty hopes that if he's around people enough without stress, maybe he could trust us enough to let us trim his hooves without having to put him in a tilt and trim."

"A tilt and trim?"

"Shy Guy won't let anyone near his legs, but when we found him, his hooves were so long he couldn't walk properly. The farrier had to bring over a tilt and trim—a metal cage we usually use on mustangs to prevent kicking—and put Shy Guy inside it, so she could turn him sideways and get to his hooves."

Hanna gazed at Shy Guy with newfound awe. "That's scary." *He must have been frightened, crammed inside a metal cage like that.*

"I doubt he was always like this. Hanoverians are usually obedient and sturdy—the Germans used them in the military and to pull coaches. You couldn't fight on a horse that spooked easy, could you?" She sighed. "I think he's just been hurt so many times he's forgotten how to trust people. Ma Etty thinks you can teach him that again, and then trimming up his hooves doesn't have to be a big event."

Hanna's eyes widened. "Me? I don't know anything about trust or horses or trimming hooves. I'm the worst person to choose!"

Madison shrugged. "Not my call. This all surprised me just as much as it did you." She stood up and handed Hanna a water bottle. "You're not a prisoner, though. Go to the bathroom, take breaks. It's hot out here. You put on sunscreen?"

Hanna rolled her eyes. "Yeah, I did. Thanks, Mom."

Madison laughed. "Okay. Remember, don't get too close to him. I mean, give him water. But even though he's pretty, I don't want you to get hurt if he spooks."

Hanna couldn't believe they had put her, of all the kids, with the dangerous horse. What kind of crazy operation was this?

But, she supposed, it sort of made sense. She was the only one not participating in riding lessons. She was deadweight. Maybe she could put her time to good use.

"Okay," said Hanna. "I understand."

\\\

So the afternoon dragged on. And the next. And the next.

Soon Shy Guy started waiting at the fence when she returned with the full bucket of water. This afternoon, he'd even stepped aside so she could push it under the bars—but when she stood back up again, he was so close that the wind blew his long, coarse forelock hair into her eyes. She didn't want to move backward too fast and surprise him, so she stood stock-still as his eyes locked with hers.

They were inches from each other, but Hanna didn't budge.

Shy Guy turned his neck so his lips brushed the metal bars. His head was so big that the space between his nostrils dwarfed her whole hand. But in his brown eyes she didn't see a horse that kicked or a horse that bit. She saw a horse that made funny faces when he wanted water and galloped through the trees at the bank of a creek for fun.

That feeling returned—that sensation of wanting to steal something, of breaking the rules, of making her own way and her own mistakes.

Remember, don't get too close to him.

Hanna raised her hand, slowly, steadily, all in Shy Guy's field of vision. He didn't move. His ears were still forward, attentive. She settled the hand on the bars, near his head. It felt right.

Safe.

His lips started to move, like he was feeling out the texture of the metal. Then his neck turned, and he ran his lips along her fingers. For a split second Hanna thought, *He could bite my fingers clean off.*

But some part of her knew that he wouldn't. So

she turned her hand to face palm up, and he ran his nose along that too.

It was velvety soft, softer than she could have imagined. Gradually, she moved her hand up his long face. He ducked his head so her hand landed on the spot between his eyes where the fur swirled like a whirlpool. Hanna rubbed under his forelock, and Shy Guy nuzzled her arm right back.

He was so soft. Each movement of his head was gentle, as if he was afraid of breaking her or scaring her off.

Hanna thought maybe they each saw the frightened creature inside the other, wanting to break out.

"I'm sorry," Hanna said to him. "I promise, whatever happened, I won't let it happen again."

\\\\\\\\\\\\\\\\\\\\\\\\\\\\\\\\\\\\\\

It was getting late in the afternoon, and the sun was sinking behind the butte when a voice called her name.

"Hanna?"

Shy Guy's head snapped up, startling her more than Madison had.

"Hanna, get down from there."

Hanna realized how precarious her position must look and climbed off the fence.

Madison was standing with her hands on her hips when Hanna landed on the ground, sending up a little dust cloud. When Madison approached, Shy Guy's ears flattened to his head and he backed away. She stopped.

"Whoa. Sorry." She eyed Hanna. "I thought I told you not to get too close."

Hanna ducked her head. "Sorry. My butt hurt from sitting on the ground, and he . . ."

"You're all right, though?"

"Yeah, I'm fine. He had an itchy head and wanted me to scratch it."

"Did he?" Madison phrased it like a question, but the corner of her mouth turned up in a slight smile. "So head scratches are a thing now?"

"I guess so."

"Cool." Madison glanced at her watch. "Well, you're off the clock. You've got an hour of free time before dinner."

"I think I'll stay here," said Hanna.

Madison frowned. "You sure? Josh is setting up the bean bag toss. He said he thought you might want to play."

Josh had said that? Hanna glanced at Shy Guy over her shoulder. He stood dispiritedly on the other side of the corral, tail flicking the air.

"I think I'm still going to stay."

Madison shrugged. "Okay. Your prerogative. I'm going to go help with dinner, so come find me if you need anything." She turned to walk away and then stopped. "Oh, and Izzy is still out in the field with Fettucini, practicing the barrel race with her free hour. In case you see a horse running around."

So Izzy was using her free hour to ride? She must be doing really well for Madison to trust her alone with her horse. Maybe she was already running barrels like a pro.

Of course a girl like Izzy would be, Hanna thought.

"Thanks," she said, climbing back up on the fence. Shy Guy came back and rested his head against the bars near her hand. Madison watched them with a smile crawling across her face.

"Have fun," she said and waved good-bye.

CHAPTER NINE

From her perch on the top bar of the corral fence, Hanna was enjoying the way the late afternoon sun turned the low-hanging clouds all sorts of pink, orange, and purple. She sat at just the perfect height to scratch between Shy Guy's ears. When someone shouted off in the distance, she didn't think twice about it—probably the ranch manager, Paul, yelling at one of his ranch hands in the milking barn across the way.

Then the shout came again, closer. Shy Guy backed away and stared at something behind Hanna.

She turned around on the metal railing and spotted Izzy, galloping toward them on her big chestnut horse. Fettucini, lathered in sweat, bumped into Hanna's knees as Izzy sidled up to her. Hanna gasped and almost fell back into the corral. And now, with Izzy in the way, she couldn't get down off the fence.

"Well, hello again, Princess Hanna," Izzy said, her huge smile making her appear extra menacing. Shy Guy snorted nervously, his ears back. "I just beat my best time on the barrels."

Hanna puckered her lips. She didn't care an inch about Izzy's barrel time.

"How's your little 'vacation' going?" asked Izzy, urging Fettucini once again closer to the corral fence. With Izzy on her horse and Hanna on the fence, they sat at the same height, and Izzy's haughty gaze met Hanna's eyes. Shy Guy paced nervously inside the corral.

"Get out of here," said Hanna, swatting at Izzy and her big red horse. She couldn't do much else from up there. "You're scaring Shy Guy."

"Oh?" Izzy leaned closer, and Hanna leaned back, feeling her balance grow unsteady. "I don't think it's him who's scared of me. I think it's you." She covered her mouth in mock surprise. "But Hanna," she cried, "I'm half your size! What are you afraid of?"

"I'm not afraid," said Hanna, but the tremble in her voice gave her away.

Izzy's grin widened. "You big wussy." With that, she reached out, put her hand on Hanna's shoulder, and shoved her backward.

Hanna's arms pinwheeled as she tried to find balance or something to hold onto, but she only grabbed open, empty air. Her riding boots flew up in front of her, and somewhere behind her, Shy Guy let out a neigh.

Her back hit the ground hard inside the corral. A searing pain shot from her hips upward, and Hanna let out a cry that was horrible even to her own ears.

Worse, she was now inside the corral—with a potentially dangerous horse. Wincing, Hanna searched for Shy Guy. Just as she turned around, huge, black hooves swung past her head. She let out a scream and rolled out of the way. Shy Guy's hooves landed with a heavy *thump*, but quickly he was galloping around the corral again, ears flattened to his skull, every muscle as tightly wound as a spring as he searched for a way out of the enclosed space. On his second pass, he almost stepped on Hanna's legs—but she tucked them under herself and rolled away again.

There wasn't enough room for both of them in here with him out of control.

"Help!" Hanna shouted at Izzy, who was scrambling off Fettucini's back. "He's going to step on me!"

"Hanna!" Izzy shouted as she sprinted to the gate. She struggled with the latch, but her movements were too panicked and it wasn't giving. Shy Guy galloped back past Hanna again, neighing frantically. Then the latch clicked, and the gate swung open.

Izzy ran inside, heedless of the huge horse making panicked circuits of the corral. She grabbed Hanna's hand and yanked her up to her feet. Behind them hooves pounded dirt, and then came a metal crash.

They turned to find the gate hanging wide open, and Shy Guy galloping away.

"No!" Hanna shouted after his retreating shape.

"Uh-oh," said Izzy, as he leapt right over the creek separating the horse barn from the rest of the ranch and took off at full tilt down Bridlemile Road.

"He's headed toward the town!"

Izzy helped Hanna limp out of the corral. None of her bones were broken, at least, but she was pretty bruised, thanks to Izzy.

But right now, that stuff didn't matter. She had to get to Shy Guy. She could only hope the ranch's front gate was closed.

"I'm going after him," said Hanna, pulling away from Izzy and stumbling.

"Are you sure you can even stand up?"

"Yeah." Hanna grunted when she put her weight on her right hip. "No thanks to you."

Izzy didn't say anything, but with tear tracks running down her cheeks, she took Fettucini by the reins. Hanna felt no sympathy.

"I'll go after him," Izzy said. "It's my fault."

Hanna was already limping off in the direction Shy Guy had run. "And bring him back how?"

"I'll get help."

"We don't have time to get help. Look! He's gone!" Shy Guy's gray shape was already disappearing behind the ranch house. Running after him on foot was pointless. At this rate, he'd make it all the way down Bridlemile Road before Hanna could catch up to him.

That was when Hanna had an idea.

"I'm going to ride with you," she told Izzy. "Get on first."

"What? You want to actually ride a horse?"

"Yes!" Hanna cried, imagining her beautiful

gray horse getting hit by a car, his heavy body collapsing lifeless to the pavement. "Now get on!"

Izzy obeyed mutely and climbed onto Fettucini's back. Then she offered one of her stirrups to Hanna.

Hanna took one, two, and then three deep breaths before she stuck her foot in the stirrup and leapt onto the horse. She landed awkwardly on the back of the saddle, and a stinging pain shot through her bruised hip. But Izzy was already turning Fettucini the way Shy Guy had gone, and she made a kissing sound with her lips.

"Hold on!" she shouted. Hanna's arms wrapped around Izzy's waist as Fettucini leapt into a gallop, taking off after Shy Guy.

They sprinted down the gravel road, Hanna barely holding on as Fettucini bumped and bounced under her. Her stomach turned with every lurch, but all she could think about was getting to Shy Guy.

Then, up ahead, she spotted him. The ranch house whizzed past. Ma Etty stepped out onto the porch, sipping her coffee, and she stared after Izzy and Hanna as they galloped by.

"Will!" she yelled behind them. "Get your horse!"

Hanna had to admit that Fettucini was fast. The three of them roared down the drive, following

Shy Guy's dust trail. Part of her thought—no, knew—that she should be afraid. But there wasn't room inside her for fear for herself. Right now, she only had space for Shy Guy. What if a truck came barreling up Bridlemile Road too fast? She could hear his bones crunching . . .

No! All Hanna could do was grit her teeth and hold on as they flew down the road, toward the front gate—which now hung wide open, the QUARTZ CREEK RANCH sign hanging over it.

"No, no, no!" cried Hanna, visualizing Shy Guy making it all the way to Main Street in Quartz Creek. But he wasn't running as fast anymore, and Fettucini easily overtook him on the straightaway.

Then Izzy and Hanna were galloping alongside him, clouds of his dust filling the air. Maybe Hanna could jump from one horse to the other, like in the movies? But that couldn't work. She'd get herself killed. But if she got off Fettucini, she couldn't keep up with the horses on foot.

A diesel engine roared up ahead. A truck was coming! Dread settled in her chest as she imagined her worst fear coming true.

But Izzy let out a whoop. "Paul!" she shouted. "We've got a runaway horse!"

A blond head in a wide-brimmed hat leaned out the window of the truck.

"Runaway?" Paul slammed on his brakes, and the truck swerved. Shy Guy stopped and reared as the truck's metal body swung around in front of them. It fishtailed, rear wheels spewing gravel until it sat stopped in the middle of the road, wedged between the fence and the creek. It wouldn't stop a horse if he was determined, but it created a small barrier.

Shy Guy neighed like a demon and reared again, sending Fettucini dancing away. Shy Guy's head craned left, then right, searching for a way past this new blockade. There was enough room at the back of the truck to slip by—and as soon as Shy Guy saw it, he lunged.

"No way!" said Izzy, reining Fettucini around to get between Shy Guy and the tail of the truck. Shy Guy backed off, throwing his head from side to side in his panic.

Paul was getting out of the truck to try to catch him with a lead rope when Shy Guy broke past the barrier Fettucini had formed with his body, knocking their legs. He dashed toward the gap between the back of the truck and the creek bed.

"No!" Hanna couldn't let him run into town,

undeterred, in this frantic and frightened state.

She jumped off Fettucini, landing with an unceremonious *thud* and a cloud of dust. Every muscle in her back and hips ached, but she ignored them. She grabbed the lead rope from Paul and jogged toward Shy Guy, even as he reared up again.

"Hey, buddy," she crooned, keeping enough distance that his flailing hooves wouldn't hit her. He landed on all four feet again and turned to look at her, ears pinned back and panting. Sweat coursed down his chest.

"Hey there," Hanna said again, in her calmest, kindest voice. "It's okay, boy. Everything will be all right."

His ears pricked slightly toward her, and his eyes followed her every step. His entire body was tensed to run, even as he looked tired, breathing heavily.

"Hanna," warned Paul. "Don't go near him. Let me—"

"I've got this," she said, still using her kindest voice. Shy Guy's gaze flicked to a point behind her, probably Paul, and his ears flattened. "Don't either of you move," she said.

"I'd listen to her," whispered Izzy.

"Hey, Shy Guy," Hanna said, earning his

attention again. She took another step toward him. "Hey, you pretty boy. See? It's okay. I'm not going to hurt you."

Shy Guy's nostrils flared, and he lifted one foot as if he might take a matching step back, but she held her hands out palms up and he stopped.

After a long moment, the only sound was Shy Guy's heavy breathing, and she took another step toward him.

"It's just me." Hanna was so close now she could smell his terrified sweat. Shy Guy shook his head, mane swishing over his huge neck. If he bolted now, he'd trample her. But if she showed fear, she would only frighten him.

Hanna had to be brave for both of them.

One more step, and she was close enough to touch him. She reached out and gently ran a hand along Shy Guy's long nose, and he seemed too tired to pull away. He whuffed, his hot breath filling her hand. Slowly she moved her hand down his neck and, fingers shaking, wrapped the lead rope around it. She tied it off in a loose knot.

"Got him," she said. Shy Guy shimmied away as Paul appeared at her shoulder, carrying a halter. He stopped mid-step.

"Maybe you should lead him back," he said quietly, handing her the halter.

"Yeah." Hanna rubbed the exhausted horse's head and neck a few more times before he was calm enough that she could buckle it over his head. He tilted his head away, but seemed too tired to fight back. She clipped on the lead rope and finally let out the breath she'd been holding.

"You did it," said Izzy, her voice surprising Hanna. She'd forgotten anyone was there but her and Shy Guy.

"Knock on wood. We still have to get back." She turned toward the ranch. Shy Guy's head hung low beside her. He was too out of energy to pull away from her as he had with Fletch.

Grasping the lead rope tightly, Hanna said, "Let's go home."

CHAPTER TEN

Hanna and Izzy walked back up Bridlemile Road, Shy Guy on Hanna's left, following along uneasily, and Izzy leading Fettucini to her right. Mr. Bridle had caught up to them on his big black horse and rode up ahead of them to make sure the way was clear. After closing the ranch gate, Paul drove behind as a blockade in case Shy Guy tried to make a break for it again. That left the two girls and their horses alone.

"Hanna . . ." Izzy trailed off. When Hanna glanced over, Izzy was fixated on her feet. "I . . . I didn't know that would happen."

"What? When you pushed me off that fence?" Keeping her voice low to avoid startling Shy Guy,

Hanna halted suddenly and turned to Izzy. The fury she'd pushed down while she focused on the rescue bubbled up, hot and fiery, to the surface. "How did you think it would turn out?"

"I don't know," said Izzy, still not looking up. "I didn't think."

"Who even does that? Pushes someone from four feet up into a corral? I could have broken my neck. Shy Guy could have trampled me. I could actually be dead right now, Izzy."

Shy Guy pulled his head away, snorting nervously at the sound of her voice.

Hanna had never been so angry in her entire life. She had disliked Izzy before, with her teasing and mocking and prancing around like she was the queen of the world. But this time, she'd gone too far.

"I'm . . . I'm sorry." Izzy's voice was so quiet, Hanna almost didn't hear her. "I'm so sorry, Hanna. I really am. I didn't mean for you to get hurt. I . . . I don't know what I was thinking. Please don't tell."

The request surprised Hanna so much, her response was a question. "Don't tell?"

"Please don't tell Madison and Ma Etty what I did. I'm in so much trouble already, you know. That's why I'm here. If my parents find out . . . if they hear I can't even stay out of trouble at a rehab camp, I'm done for. They were already threatening to make me change schools."

"But . . ."

Izzy covered her face in her hands and tears dripped out, down her chin, onto the dirt. "Please! I'll make it up to you. I promise." Shy Guy fidgeted at her wail.

They needed to keep moving and keep it down if they were going to get Shy Guy home safely, so Hanna let out a sigh. "Okay, fine. I won't tell."

Izzy dropped her hands to her sides and relief flooded her face.

"But don't think it means I've forgiven you. You put my life at risk for a . . . what? A joke? That's hard to forget."

Izzy nodded. "I understand. I promise I'll make it up to you."

Hanna wasn't sure what to make of the determination in Izzy's voice, but as they approached the ranch house and she saw Ma Etty waiting for them, she felt a little hopeful.

Or maybe it was the adrenaline.

After Hanna had returned Shy Guy to his corral, Ma Etty told her to come inside.

"That was incredibly reckless, Hanna Abbott," she said, hands perched on her hips.

Hanna winced at her full name.

The ranch house was abuzz with news of Shy Guy's flight—and the maneuver that saved him. But Ma Etty had ushered everyone out of the living room except for the two girls in question.

Before Hanna could say anything, Izzy pushed in, physically standing between Hanna and Ma Etty.

"Hanna did the best she could, given the situation," said Izzy. "If we hadn't done something, Shy Guy would be roadkill!"

This made both Hanna and Ma Etty flinch.

Still. Of all people, it was Izzy defending her. Hanna didn't know what to make of that.

Ma Etty surveyed them. "You could have asked someone for help," she said. "Leaping onto a horse when you've never received even basic riding lessons . . ."

"We had to act fast," said Hanna. "If we'd had time, I promise, I would've way preferred to ask for help instead."

Paul leaned his head out the dining room doorway. "I don't know what you're lecturing her for, Ma

Etty," he said, his bushy blond mustache twitching. "That girl handled that horse incredibly well in a difficult situation, especially for a newbie."

Ma Etty frowned. "I didn't ask you, Paul."

"Well, that's true," he responded good-naturedly, "but isn't she the one that's scared to even get near a horse?" He tilted his head at Hanna.

"Yes," Ma Etty allowed.

"Pretty remarkable what she did, then, isn't it? Riding double your first time on a horse!"

Ma Etty didn't say anything, but her gaze went to Hanna.

"She didn't want to do it," said Izzy, breaking the silence. "But she had to!"

"Now, now," said Ma Etty, putting her hands up. "There are always options."

"There wasn't one this time." Izzy crossed her arms. "Hanna's the only one Shy Guy will let anywhere near him. It was a good thing she was brave enough to ride after him with me, because nobody else would've been able to get a halter on him."

Even though she was the one on trial, Hanna didn't dare interject—Izzy was handling it better than she would've.

"It was still a pretty dangerous thing to do, for

someone who's never ridden before," said Ma Etty. "I don't want anyone to get hurt on my watch. You didn't even have a helmet!"

Izzy gaped at her. "What? You can't be mad at Hanna for that. The scaredy-cat actually rode a horse! You should be happy."

Now, Ma Etty looked more confused than angry. She tilted her head at Izzy.

"And that makes me wonder. How did all this happen in the first place?"

Izzy and Hanna exchanged a glance. It was Hanna's turn to hold up her end of the bargain. She wished she'd worked on an excuse earlier.

"Shy Guy got out," she said lamely.

"How?"

Hanna opened and closed her mouth. This was the same thing that had happened when her mom found the stash of stolen stuff under her bed and demanded to know what she was doing. Hanna wasn't imaginative enough for good excuses.

"It was an accident," chimed in Izzy. "The gate wasn't latched properly."

Hanna nodded along. "Yep. And when Izzy came over with Fettucini to say hello, Shy Guy got scared and ran."

"To say hello?" Ma Etty surveyed both girls like a detective examining two suspects.

"Right," said Izzy. "You know, because . . . because Hanna and I have been hanging out a lot!" She flopped on the couch next to Hanna and put her in a headlock.

"Have you?" said Ma Etty, her surprise genuine this time.

"Y-yeah," managed Hanna, forcing herself to smile as she pushed Izzy off. "We have. All the time."

"We even came up with a joke," said Izzy. "Why didn't the horse speak?"

Hanna gave her a blank look. "Uh . . . why?"

"Because he was a little hoarse!"

Nobody laughed at the lame joke except Izzy, but Ma Etty did crack a smile. "Well, that's good to hear. But I'm still not happy with how reckless you were—riding double, leaving the property without permission . . ."

"We had to think fast," said Izzy. "We made a snap decision, and I stand by it."

"A decision that could have saved Shy Guy's life," chimed in Paul. Ma Etty gave him an annoyed look for his continued interference. "Even if she did get a little beat up."

Ma Etty's eyes narrowed. "Yeah, Hanna. How are you feeling? Neither of you has explained how Hanna got all covered in dirt."

Paul gave them a sheepish look and withdrew back into the dining room.

"I fell," said Hanna. "It was . . . before Shy Guy got out."

"Mm-hmm." Ma Etty didn't sound convinced, but when no one opted to explain further, she let out a defeated sigh. She did look pleased, though, to see the two girls sitting on the couch together. "Well, nobody's in trouble here, I suppose. Everyone did what they could in a bad situation and made it work." She nodded in Hanna's direction. "But you should be more careful. Remember, Shy Guy has had a hard time in life. You can't always trust him."

Hanna closed her eyes. "I know. But I think . . . I think he could be trusted again. He's a good horse, Ma Etty, but he's been hurt a lot."

"He was letting you scratch him," said Izzy. "Nobody could do that before, right, Ma Etty?"

Hanna shrugged. "I think he just knows I won't hurt him."

Ma Etty's smile widened. "I'm glad we paired you two up, then. He needs someone like you."

CHAPTER ELEVEN

The next morning, Madison told them at breakfast that Fletch would be working with Izzy, Rae Ann, Cade, and Josh so she could give Hanna a private lesson. Hanna waited for a snide remark from Izzy about getting more special treatment. But Izzy kept eating, even catching Hanna's eye and smiling lopsidedly.

Dumbfounded, Hanna missed her mouth with a forkful of eggs and spilled it right down her shirt.

After they broke up for riding instruction, Hanna met Madison by the corral.

"Normally we start everyone with the basics," she said. "We call it 'groundwork'—you know, how to handle the horse, lead it, and ask it to wait. Like heeling a dog. I want to teach you how to do it correctly right from the beginning so Shy Guy knows he can't get away with any fooling around on your watch. Given we can even get that far." Madison held out a pretty green halter to Hanna. "I think green is Shy Guy's color," she said with a grin.

Hanna took it, put it over her own shoulder, and shivered. She'd had no problem putting a halter on Shy Guy yesterday, when his life was at stake. It had been instinct.

She'd felt superhuman.

But now, with the halter in her hand, fear whistled through her blood. Madison had . . . expectations. Groundwork? Bossing around a horse?

Hanna couldn't do that. Hanna didn't know how to boss around anyone. Who would listen to her, anyway? Certainly not a big horse like Shy Guy.

"One thing," said Madison. "Remember to listen to everything I say. If it feels like Shy Guy might act up, I want you to drop the lead rope and get away as quickly as possible."

"You think that might . . . happen?" Hanna shivered.

"I don't know," said Madison. "I really don't. But I'd rather be safe than sorry."

Shy Guy stood peacefully in the middle of the corral, facing away from the gate. When they approached him from behind, he raised his head and pinned his ears back—until he spotted Hanna. Turning completely around, his ears pricked toward her.

Hanna walked up to the fence, and slowly, he walked forward to meet her. She patted his nose through the bars, and he let out a soft whuff.

"All right," said Madison, sounding like she'd been holding her breath. "We'll start with opening and closing the gate. We want Shy Guy to wait behind the gate while you open it and go in."

"Go in?" said Hanna. She had thought they would work somewhere a little less . . . enclosed.

"Yep. Just say, 'wait,' and hold the halter and lead rope in your hand. Shake the rope at him to ask him to move back. Don't open the gate until he's standing at attention and giving you plenty of space."

Hanna stared up at Shy Guy. He stared back at her through the fence. Carrying the halter, she made her way around the corral to the gate. He followed her every movement with his ears. Once she was at the gate, she said, "Wait."

Shy Guy stepped up to the gate and poked his nose through it, wanting her to pet him again. "No, silly boy. Go back." His ears flicked up at the command.

"Shake the lead rope a little," said Madison.

"Go back," Hanna said again, giving the rope the tiniest of shakes, scared she might frighten him if she shook it too hard.

But Shy Guy, head lowering, took a step backward. A surge of pride rushed through her.

Madison made an impressed noise. "Wow. I guess he's been trained by somebody along the way."

"You didn't know?"

"Nope. We had a hunch because of his breed—Hanoverians are usually dressage and jumping horses—but no one's been able to tell until now. Okay, now unlatch the gate and go inside."

Hanna's heart sped up. Reaching for the latch, she lifted it, and the gate opened a little. "Make sure he stays back," Madison said.

But Hanna didn't have to tell Shy Guy. He stood patiently a short distance away as she went inside and closed the gate behind her. She could practically feel Madison's anxiety on the other side of the fence.

Hanna was inside the corral with Shy Guy again.

Last time they were here, he almost took her head off. But he didn't move a muscle as she approached him with the halter.

"Now put the front strap of the halter up and over his nose," said Madison, voice barely loud enough to avoid startling Shy Guy. "I wish I could be in there to show you, but I don't think he'd allow it."

"That's okay," said Hanna. "I did it the other day. I remember how." And something told her he wasn't ready to engage with other people yet. He still couldn't be trusted.

Could she even trust him?

The thought flitted through her head so fast it was gone before she could think too hard about it. Hanna focused on bringing the halter strap up behind Shy Guy's ears slowly, so he wouldn't spook, and then buckling it. When she was done, she gently patted the side of his head and he snorted.

"Great job," breathed Madison, unclenching her hands, which had been gripping the metal bars. Her knuckles were white. "Now take the lead rope and lead him around the corral."

To both of their surprise, Shy Guy not only obeyed Hanna's commands, but with Madison doling out instructions, he didn't shy or balk. For all Hanna's novice guiding, Shy Guy knew exactly what he was doing. He stopped when she stopped, maintaining a polite distance. When she turned, he followed, and never pushed or tried to get ahead of her. He backed up at the word *back*. She didn't even have to shake the rope.

"Wow," Hanna heard Madison mutter to herself. "I'm sorry I doubted you, boy."

Eventually, after what felt like a long lesson, Madison stopped her. "Let's call it good while we're ahead. Looks like the tables got turned on me today. Shy Guy gave us a schooling in manners." She shook her head in amazement.

"Do you think he's ready to go in the barn yet?" asked Hanna. The successful lesson left her feeling rather bold. "I feel sorry for him, sitting in this corral alone all day."

Madison's eyebrows rose to her hairline. "I don't know, Hanna. Last time we tried to take him in there, he almost took off Mr. Bridle's arm trying to get away."

Hanna glanced at Shy Guy's gray coat, which was dusty and brown in splotches after all his sweating and running. The locks of hair around his ankles were matted together with mud.

"He's also really dirty," Hanna pointed out.

"Oh man." Madison nervously retied her pony-tail, the same way Hanna did. A resigned sigh escaped her lips. "I suppose we could try. But if he spooks or tries to run, let him go. I made sure the ranch gate was closed this morning."

"Okay," said Hanna. "I will."

Madison shook her head, like she couldn't believe she'd given in. "All right, first things first. Bring him to the gate. Then ask him to wait while you open it. Once you're outside, ask him to walk through, and close it behind you."

Hanna led Shy Guy to the gate, where she lifted the latch and pulled it open. She stepped through and then gestured for Shy Guy to follow. He dipped his head and walked through and turned to face her as she closed the gate behind them. She felt so victorious at the smooth, clean way they moved together that after the gate latched closed, she swung one arm up in the air and clenched her fist.

"Yeah!" she cheered.

Shy Guy threw his head back violently, yanking the lead rope out of Hanna's hand. When Madison jumped over to try to grab the spinning lead rope, he let out a frightened squeal and danced out of her range.

"Wait!" Hanna held up a hand. Madison immediately stopped moving. When she did, Shy Guy settled back down on four legs, breathing hard. "Just wait," Hanna told her. "It's all right." Giving him a moment to calm down, she calmly stepped toward Shy Guy and took the lead rope again.

"I'm sorry," she said, offering the offending hand for him to smell, to remember it wouldn't hurt him. When he didn't move away, she gently ran her hand down his nose. "I didn't mean to frighten you."

But her swinging arm had reminded him—it had brought him back to a time when he was trained, when he had been perfect, and someone had hurt him anyway. Hanna's heart ached.

Madison, taking careful, small steps, came up beside her. Shy Guy eyed her but didn't retreat.

"It's going to be a long, slow road," Madison said, holding out her own hand for him to smell. He jerked his head back, but when Madison didn't fight him or try to tug him closer, Shy Guy eventually stuck out his nose to smell her. After many long seconds, he ran his lips over her hand. Madison jerked back at first but Hanna shook her head.

"Don't worry. He does that when he wants you to pet him."

Even Madison was frightened of Shy Guy? The horse trainer steeled herself, reached out, and ran her palm over the velvety skin of Shy Guy's nose. He nuzzled her back.

Madison's face melted. "Oh, wow. He's soft."

"Isn't he?"

The moments drifted past, the three of them standing in silence while Madison petted Shy Guy. As his eyes closed and he leaned in to her scratches, Madison's eyes filled with unshed tears.

"Let's wait to do the barn tomorrow," she said after a while, her voice catching. "One victory at a time."

CHAPTER TWELVE

After another lesson on groundwork the next day, Madison suggested they take Shy Guy into the barn.

"You're right," she told Hanna. "He could use a good grooming."

Shy Guy put up some resistance at first, but with a full bucket of grain luring him in and Hanna at his side, Shy Guy eventually gave in.

Once they had him in cross ties, Madison talked Hanna through brushing. Starting at his neck with a curry comb, Hanna worked her way down his side, sweeping it in a circular motion. Once she'd stirred up all the dirt, Hanna traded the curry comb for the softer bristle brush. One flick at a time, his muddy gray coat turned silver and glossy until, even under the dim barn lights, he simply glowed.

For a long while, the two girls stared at Shy Guy in awe.

"Dang," said Madison. "That is one fine-looking horse."

Next, it was time to pick his hooves. Hanna had seen the other kids pick their horses' hooves before, and it required holding the horse's hoof close enough to your body to dig out whatever was stuck inside it—which was right inside kicking range.

"You'll be fine," said Madison, with a confidence Hanna did not feel. "It's one of the most essential parts of grooming, as well as trust building. Plus, he needs it. I bet his feet hurt."

Well, then, Hanna decided—she'd do it. She followed Madison's coaching, running her hand down the back of Shy Guy's leg, which, surprisingly, he didn't mind at all. He nudged Hanna's back with his nose, startling her. Was he playing with her?

Sure enough, his hooves were packed full of mud, sand, and even a few large rocks. "Poor Shy Guy," Hanna murmured. She went from hoof to hoof, and to both her and Madison's amazement, he obeyed without question. Hanna hardly had to apply pressure to his ankle—Madison called it his fetlock—to get him to lift it.

When she was done cleaning the final hoof, she set it back down on the ground. Shy Guy put his weight on it, testing it. His body relaxed noticeably, and he nudged Hanna again, as if to say thank you.

"So well-mannered," breathed Madison. "Where did you come from, Shy Guy?"

\\

Hanna floated on clouds the rest of the day. She hardly remembered the milking lesson that Paul gave them in the cattle barn. When they had free time, Josh invited Hanna to play the bean bag toss with him.

"How's the troubled horse rehab going?" he asked her.

Hanna couldn't help but laugh. "Troubled youth in rehab meets troubled horse in rehab. Never thought about it like that before. But Shy Guy's coming along."

"You make a good pair." He threw his bean bag and completely missed. "Dang," he said. "Didn't realize I was so bad at this when I invited you to play."

"No, it's great," said Hanna with a chuckle. "Keep making throws like that. I like winning."

Josh gave a sheepish smile.

"Usually, I'm a pretty good shot," he said, collecting the bean bags. "You'd never guess, but I play baseball."

"You're right! I wouldn't guess."

Hanna was glad Josh's big laugh showed he hadn't taken her seriously. In the waning afternoon sun, they played until Hanna thought her arm would fall off.

That night in the girls' cabin, they read on their bunk beds in silence until it was time for lights-out.

"Tomorrow we'll do something more exciting with Shy Guy," Madison promised Hanna.

"More exciting?" She wasn't sure she liked the sound of that. "I liked what we did today."

"Good. But there's so much more to horsemanship. From what I saw out there, someone has trained Shy Guy very well." Madison balled one hand into a fist and looked up at the ceiling, like a coach in a football movie who's just found inspiration. "I wish it could be me, Hanna, but you're the one he's chosen to open up to. I have a feeling that if we go slowly, you'll discover some amazing things about that horse."

The lights clicked off, but Hanna lay awake for some time thinking about what Madison had said.

Shy Guy had done so well today—he was obviously a great horse underneath his fear, and eager to please. But what would taking the next step require Hanna to do?

\\\

They did more groundwork the next day. And the next. Then one morning, after the other kids had already saddled up and gone outside, Madison stopped Hanna before she could lead Shy Guy out of the barn.

"I want to try something new today," she said cautiously. "What do you say we get a saddle on him?"

Hanna's gut did a leapfrog over her heart.

"You want me to ride?" she asked, her voice more of a squeak.

Madison shook her head. "No, no. Don't worry— this is just a small step to get Shy Guy accustomed to the saddle again. We can't catapult straight into riding. Neither of you are ready for that, anyway."

Hanna could feel she was still making a worried face.

"Seriously," said Madison, half laughing. She patted Hanna's shoulder. "Let's start with a saddle blanket."

Madison vanished into the tack room and returned with a thick, green blanket that matched Shy Guy's green halter.

"It happens this one's the right size," she said, winking. Hanna liked him in that deep, emerald green. Standing a safe distance from the horse, Madison set the blanket on a saddle rack. "Now, this may be a bit tricky, Hanna, if he has bad associations with the saddle—which he likely does after the saddle sores we found on him."

Hanna understood. Lifting the blanket off the rack, she carried it over to Shy Guy.

His ears pricked toward her, and she held out the blanket for him to smell. His head jerked away, nostrils flaring, and the lead rope snapped tight.

Suddenly the space in the barn became very small. What if he tried to bolt?

"It's okay, boy," said Hanna, taking the blanket away again.

"Here," said Madison, dumping a handful of horse treats in Hanna's hand. "Try giving him one of these while you let him smell it. Positive reinforcement!"

It was worth a try. With a treat in one hand,

Hanna held out the blanket again for Shy Guy's inspection. He sniffed the blanket for only a second before smelling the offered treat and lipping it up.

"Now, slowly, touch his side with it," said Madison. "Get him used to how it feels. Stay by his shoulder."

Holding the blanket in clear sight, Hanna took a step down Shy Guy's side and held it out so the edge barely touched him. She moved the blanket back and forth a little, so he could get a good sense of the texture and fabric. His ears flattened against his head.

"Give him another treat," encouraged Madison. Shy Guy lipped Hanna's hand before eating the treat out of her palm. His ears relaxed, and Hanna lifted the blanket higher on his back.

"Can you give him the treat so I can use both hands?" Hanna asked. "The blanket's too bulky."

Again, the nervousness on Madison's face surprised Hanna. But she held out the treat to Shy Guy and he slurped it up as Hanna slid the blanket over his back. His ears flicked in her direction, but that was all.

Hanna let out a heavy breath. "Wow," she said. "All that to get the blanket on?"

"I know it doesn't look like much, but this is a big step for Shy Guy. We couldn't even get a brush near him before."

\\

After taking the blanket off, they worked with Shy Guy in the corral.

"Trust building," Madison told her. "One step at a time."

Every day, they put the saddle blanket on and took it off again, until Shy Guy stopped putting up a fuss. Then Madison dragged a saddle out of the tack room.

First, she demonstrated putting a saddle on her smaller Appaloosa horse, Snow White, so Hanna could see how it was done.

Adjusting Shy Guy to the saddle was easier than adjusting him to the blanket. Even when the saddle settled on Shy Guy's back, he appeared only mildly irritated. It wasn't until she tightened the cinch that he went over the edge.

Shy Guy broke free of her grasp, and arching his back, he jumped a foot straight up in the air. Hanna yelped. Madison pulled her out of the way as he crow-hopped again, almost running into the barn wall.

"Shy Guy!" Hanna squeaked. She wanted to pet him, to calm him down, but Madison kept her back.

"Let him work it out."

Shy Guy hopped side to side, desperate to get the saddle off—but it wouldn't budge. Soon he gave up and settled for standing uncomfortably with his ears pressed back, his tail flicking in obvious irritation, like a cat.

"Well, that's good progress considering where we started," said Madison.

"Why did he do that?"

She shook her head sadly. "Someone worked him hard with a saddle that didn't fit—probably didn't brush him down properly either. Every time he wore that saddle, it rubbed until his skin was raw."

Hanna wanted to take the saddle off him right then. "Is it hurting him now?"

"Oh, no. But now he associates the cinch tightening with pain to come, even if there isn't any. We just have to show him we know what we're doing." Madison pointed off to the other arena. "Let's go walk him around a bit and see how those other goofballs are doing."

Leading Shy Guy in a halter, the saddle still

on his back, they walked along the outside of the practice ring where Fletch was working with the other four kids. "Izzy!" he shouted as Izzy galloped past him. "Stop running around. We're trying to do an exercise here."

"Poor Fletch." Madison shook her head. "Izzy's enough to handle all on her own." When the other kids spotted Hanna and Shy Guy, they stopped what they were doing.

"Hey, Hanna!" Josh waved. "Looking great."

Hanna had no idea if he meant her or her horse, so she just smiled and waved back.

Izzy and Fettucini jogged over, making Shy Guy dance away from the fence.

"Izzy, don't scare him," called Fletch.

"Sorry!" Izzy reined in Fettucini, and the gelding patiently stepped back from the fence. "That's cool that you got a saddle on him."

"Yep," said Hanna, running a hand down Shy Guy's neck to calm him down. Once he was settled, she continued walking him along the fence line.

"Izzy, can you leave them alone?" asked Fletch, not trying to hide the impatience in his voice. "They're doing important training."

Disappointment settled on Izzy's small features.

"Okay, fine," she said, turning Fettucini back toward the others and trotting over to where they had lined up to practice the keyhole event.

Taking her turn, Rae Ann slowly walked her horse over to the four poles arranged in a square, passed into the middle, turned around, and walked out again.

"Come on, Rae Ann," said Fletch, sounding exasperated. "You can trot through it, at least. You're allowed to trot."

"I don't like trotting." Her stocky bay horse didn't much look like it liked trotting either.

"Sorry, Fletch!" Madison called to him, though her grin didn't make her appear sorry. "I think Hanna and Shy Guy could be ready to join the group sometime soon."

Hanna's head shot up. "Really?" she asked as they headed back to the barn. Shy Guy snorted. "You think we'll be ready?" She half wanted to hear Madison say *yes* and half wanted to hear *no*.

"I sure do," said Madison.

CHAPTER THIRTEEN

Hanna got garden duty again that afternoon, but when she showed up with her water bottle and trowel at the garden, it wasn't Josh who was waiting for her.

It was Izzy.

When Hanna stepped into the dirt, Izzy shot up to her feet and shoved both her hands behind her back.

"Hey, Hanna!" she chirped, too brightly.

"Hey," Hanna said, putting down her water bottle. What was Izzy up to now? "What'cha got there?" she asked.

Izzy glanced around like Hanna meant something other than what she was holding behind her back. "What do you mean?"

"I mean, what are you hiding behind your back, Izzy?"

Izzy's eyes darkened and a shiver ran up Hanna's spine.

"Nothing," she said quickly. "Gotta go. I have to use the bathroom."

"But we just got here." They stared at each other for a long moment. Then, with a defeated sigh, Izzy extended her right hand and opened it.

Lying in her palm was a phone and a pair of tangled earbuds.

"You're not supposed to have any electronics," Hanna said.

"I know. That's why I was hiding it, dork." Izzy rolled her eyes. "It doesn't get service out here, but I really wanted to listen to the Lawnchairs. I used to play them all the time when I gardened with my dad."

"The Lawnchairs?" Hanna took the player and earbuds before Izzy could hide them again. "You know them?"

"What? And you do?"

"Yeah. Of course." How could Izzy possibly know the Lawnchairs too? "They're a little band out of my hometown."

Izzy gaped at her. "You're from Sturgis?"

"Yeah. I didn't think anyone else outside of Sturgis knew they existed. It's the same band, right? Maybe there are two with the same name."

"Nope." Izzy fervently shook her head. "The two girls, right? One does keyboard and sings. The other does guitar."

"Oh man, Noelle can shred! You know that song by them, 'Bonfire'?"

Izzy's face lit up. "Yeah! 'Bonfire' is one of my favorites! I heard it at my friend's house once, and I've loved them since." She pointed at herself. "Diehard fan."

"No way," Hanna breathed. "That's wild. I didn't know anyone else had even heard of them."

"Well, I have."

Hanna popped in one earbud and offered Izzy the other. Surprised, she took it and put it in her ear.

"Press PLAY," Izzy said. "I was only on the first song of the album."

When she tapped the screen, lyrics belted into Hanna's ear. "Mariah has such a cool voice," she murmured.

"I know. She can go so low! She sounds like a dude sometimes."

"Right? It's awesome." The guitar swelled and then gave way to keyboard synths.

"Here," said Izzy, taking the phone and changing the song. "'Bonfire' is great, don't get me wrong, but this is actually my favorite song on this album."

A song came on that Hanna hadn't heard in ages—not since that first day she stole something, when she took that first stolen candy bar out of her pocket. Hanna hadn't even wanted to eat it. She just enjoyed getting away with it. She'd thought, *This is the worst thing I could possibly do. If Mom found out, she'd never get on my case for something stupid ever again.*

After that, she'd done it a second time. And a third. At the grocery store, in a gas station. What Hanna loved most was operating right under her mom's nose, knowing how much she'd flip if she found out.

Izzy was watching Hanna's face carefully when the song ended.

"You're not going to tell on me, are you?" she asked. "For having the phone?"

"Is that why you were hiding it?"

"Duh. You already have dirt on me from when I . . ." Izzy stopped, pressing her lips together in a hard line. "Well, you know."

Right. When she almost got Hanna killed.

"Please don't tell," said Izzy. "I'm sure Madison would tell my parents, and they'd shake their heads just like they do when I come home with a pink slip."

"You get in trouble a lot?" asked Hanna.

Izzy shrugged. "I guess. My teachers in Arizona are dumb and so is everyone else at school. So I tell them that. And sometimes follow it up with a punch. I mean, not the teachers. Yet."

"Wow," said Hanna, eyes widening. Izzy was small, but Hanna still wouldn't want a fist in the face from her.

"But why?" Hanna asked. "Doesn't punching someone kinda . . . hurt? And don't you get in trouble?"

"If you do it wrong, it hurts," said Izzy. "And whatever. I didn't mind the pink slips that much."

"You like getting in trouble?"

"Sure. Sometimes. I have three sisters. Sometimes putting a pink slip in front of my dad is the only way to get his attention for more than five seconds."

Hanna understood that feeling more than she was willing to admit.

She could tell on Izzy for the phone. Hanna liked Ma Etty and Madison and everyone else, and disobeying their rules didn't sit well. But something about Izzy smuggling this in, right under everyone's noses, to listen to her favorite band—well, it was brave.

Plus, Hanna really liked the Lawnchairs.

"Well," she said, tapping her chin. "I guess I won't tell. But only if you let me listen in while we pull these weeds."

Izzy's smile was huge and white and bright as the sun. Hanna couldn't help smiling back.

"Okay," Izzy agreed. "Keep an eye out for anyone coming to check on us, though."

"All right." They stooped in the dirt and scooted closer together so they could share the earbuds. Then Izzy pressed PLAY on the next song.

They listened to the album three times through before the sun dipped behind the mountains and Madison called them in for dinner.

\\\\\\\\\\\\\\\\\\\\\\\\\\\\\\\\\\\\\\\

Hanna and Madison repeated the process of getting Shy Guy used to the blanket—but with the saddle. They put on the saddle, tightened the cinch, and waited while Shy Guy bucked out his anxiety. Then they walked him around before taking it off again.

After a week of this, he endured saddling with far less fuss. The day that he accepted the saddle without even pinning his ears back, Madison suggested they start out learning how to put on a bridle with an easier horse.

"I want you to try it a few times on Lacey and get it right before attempting to put a bridle on Shy Guy," she told Hanna as they entered the barn. "Think you can handle it?"

Hanna considered it. Already this summer, she'd fallen into a corral with a huge, frightened, stampeding horse. She'd ridden emergency double with Izzy, of all people. Hanna could put a bridle on a little sleepy pony like Lacey.

Sure enough, Lacey practically slept through it. When Hanna had successfully gotten the bridle on and off twice by herself, she realized she'd done the whole thing without any trepidation at all.

Madison clapped her on the shoulder and said, "Great job. I think you've got the nuts and bolts. Let's try it on our guy."

Once they'd put Lacey away, Hanna went to Shy Guy's stall door and lifted the green halter off the hook. He snorted and excitedly thrust his head toward her over the door.

"He's always so excited to see us," said Hanna, giving in to Shy Guy's demands for scratches.

"It's probably been a long time since a human treated him as well as you do."

After Hanna took him out of the stall, they went through the saddle routine again. Then it was time for the bridle.

Hanna walked through the steps of removing the halter. She let Shy Guy smell the leather reins of the bridle before putting them over his neck. When it came time to put the bit in his mouth, Hanna faltered. Getting her hands close to Lacey's mouth hadn't bothered her—Lacey didn't have a history of biting.

"You can do it," urged Madison. What if he didn't open for it? She didn't want to put her fingers in his mouth to make him open.

Taking a deep breath, Hanna pressed the bit to Shy Guy's lips.

His mouth opened immediately.

Hanna pushed the bit inside and pulled the bridle up and over his ears. When it was secure, she buckled the chin strap.

"Whew," she said, wiping her forehead.

"See?" said Madison. "No problem. Let's walk

him around again. Then we'll do some exercises in the corral to get him moving a little. He could use it." Without thinking about it, Madison patted Shy Guy's belly.

He let out a squeal and swung his body away, knocking over the wooden saddle stand. Hanna jumped and Madison stepped back, saying, "Whoa! Whoa, boy."

Hanna was shaking when Shy Guy, breathing hard, finally settled down.

Madison looked positively ashamed. "Sorry about that," she said, righting the saddle stand. "It's easy to forget since you started working with Shy Guy that he's still afraid of most people."

When her heartbeat returned to normal, Hanna picked up the fallen reins.

"No problem," she said. They all stood quietly, letting the charge of the moment drain away.

"You know, though," Madison said quietly, "he's come really far." She turned to Hanna. "And so have you. Do you think you're ready for your first riding lesson tomorrow?"

Hanna's stomach sank like a stone tossed in a lake. "R-riding lesson?"

Riding was what they'd been preparing for, after

all. She imagined sitting astride magnificent Shy Guy, galloping down a quiet country road, his silver hair flowing in the same wind as her blonde hair.

But in the same daydream, something startled him, and he reared up, beating the air with his hooves, tossing Hanna from his back like a sack of potatoes.

Shy Guy wouldn't hurt her intentionally, she reminded herself. But could she trust him anyway?

Madison looked reassuring. "Your first few lessons won't be on Shy Guy, of course. We'll start you on Lacey till you're more comfortable in the saddle."

Hanna couldn't speak.

"Think about it, and you can decide tomorrow," said Madison. "That horse has made a lot of progress, but you're the only person he trusts. I don't mean to pressure you—it's your choice, Hanna—but if anyone's going to be able to ride him again, it'll be you."

No pressure, indeed. Hanna tried to swallow the tight lump that had formed in her throat, but failed.

Hanna!

It was her mom's voice.

Hanna, honey, why are you crying?

You've always loved horses. I don't understand.

Hanna, please. You're embarrassing me.
It's not time to get off the horses yet.
Hanna.
Please.
Stop crying.

CHAPTER FOURTEEN

Around the dinner table everyone but Hanna was in a good mood, swapping funny vacation stories over Mr. Bridle's "famous" eggplant lasagna. Hanna brooded as she picked apart the slippery layers of noodles.

Madison was right. Shy Guy didn't trust anyone else. And Hanna couldn't very well ask Madison to try him out first—she could get hurt. Hanna had to learn how to ride.

"Eggplant not your thing?" Ma Etty asked, startling Hanna.

"No, no," she said, and made a point of taking a big bite. "The eggplant's fine. I'm not that hungry."

"What are you thinking about?" Ma Etty asked.

Hanna let out a stuttering breath. "Madison wants me to ride tomorrow. But . . ." She dropped her fork to her plate. "I don't think I can do it."

"What do you mean?" Ma Etty shot her a look of pure surprise. "Of course you can."

"What if I get thrown? What if—"

"Did what-ifs stop you when Shy Guy got out of the corral?"

"No."

"Then why let nerves stop you this time? Shy Guy needs you as much now as he did then."

Hanna's brow creased. "Needs me?"

"Absolutely," said Ma Etty. "Everyone deserves a second chance—even Shy Guy. Especially Shy Guy. He has so much potential. How sad would it be if he was never ridden again? If he spent the rest of his days in a pasture—exercised occasionally in a pen and otherwise forgotten about?"

Hanna hadn't thought of it like that. She'd been so focused on herself, on her own fears and well-being, that she hadn't considered how Shy Guy must feel. He was so well-trained, so eager to please. What a shame to waste a great horse.

"I just don't know," said Hanna. The time she'd

ridden Fettucini had been an emergency.

This wasn't. And she was scared.

"Get a feel for the saddle with Lacey tomorrow," said Ma Etty. "And give it some thought. Seems to me that you're Shy Guy's best chance to be the horse we both know he can be."

\\

The whole walk from the ranch house to the barn the next morning, Hanna kept reminding herself: *I'm giving Shy Guy a second chance. I'm learning to ride for his sake.*

"So let's talk about mounting," said Madison, once they'd gotten little Lacey out of her stall. "You always want to mount on the left. She should stand still for you—if she starts to move, stop and resituate her before you try getting on again. Put one foot in the stirrup and pull yourself up by the horn."

Trying to remember all of these instructions, Hanna walked around Lacey's front so she was standing on her left side. Taking a deep breath, she put one hand on the horn, one foot in the stirrup, and hauled herself up into the seat.

Lacey yawned.

Hanna settled into the saddle and was surprised to find the fear she'd expected had dulled and faded, like well-worn jeans.

Madison passed Hanna the reins. "Okay. Let's start real easy, with a walk, and we'll go from there."

\\

The landscape of the ranch changed dramatically atop a horse. The sun shone brighter, and the pasture spread out even farther, like a green shag carpet. Even that big, lumpy butte took on a shimmery halo during Hanna's morning riding lessons.

Riding turned out to be far less stressful than she'd expected. Then again, riding Lacey was a bit like sitting in the car when her grandmother drove. Slow, steady, and kind of boring.

Madison never pressured her to do more than she could. Hanna could get off whenever she wanted. The first time they tried a trot, the fast bouncing frightened Hanna so much that she had to have Madison help her off the horse's back. She stood, shaking, until she grew calm enough to try again.

After another circuit of the corral, bouncing crazily, Hanna decided she didn't particularly like the trot.

"Don't hold onto the horn," Madison kept telling her. "You're not going to fall off!"

"I feel like I am!" Hanna would shout back.

Over the next few days, Hanna learned how to turn, back up, and ask for a trot and a canter, all while they worked on her posture and control. The lessons were intensive, but Hanna was determined to become the best rider she could for Shy Guy.

After her lesson every day, though she was tired from riding and brushing down Lacey and putting her away, Hanna and Madison would still tack up and work out Shy Guy in the corral. Madison taught her how to use the longe line to exercise him, and they discovered that Shy Guy understood every verbal command that Madison had stored up.

Madison shook her head. "I can't tell if it's him or the Hanoverian in him," she said.

"What?"

"He's perfectly obedient. He'll do whatever you ask, when you ask it." Madison shook her head. "I'll never understand why someone hit a horse like Shy Guy. Honestly."

Hanna didn't either.

After a week of longeing Shy Guy almost every day, Madison said, "How about tomorrow?"

"What about tomorrow?" asked Hanna.

"I think it's time to try riding him. So how about tomorrow?"

Right. The real test and the reason for all this.

"Think about it," Madison said. "But in my professional opinion, you're both ready to try."

Hanna made herself nod, but she couldn't even force out a *yes*.

\\\

Breakfast the next day was a blur. Rae Ann moaned about missing her cat back in Vermont. Josh and Cade were arguing about video games. Hanna wasn't listening. Instead, she was chewing one of her nails down to the bed when someone tapped her on the shoulder.

"You okay?" It was Izzy, collecting dishes. "You're white in the face. I mean, uh, whiter than usual."

Hanna couldn't help but laugh at that. It came out tremulous and shaky.

"I'm thinking."

Izzy scooped up her dish. "About what?"

Why did she want to know? "I'm going to ride Shy Guy today," said Hanna.

The dishes clattered as Izzy almost dropped them. "Whoa. That's a big step."

"I know."

"Here, I gotta go put these in the kitchen, but wait up for me." Before Hanna could say anything, Izzy twirled and flew away, making a ruckus in the kitchen as she deposited the dishes.

"It's your day to load the dishwasher, Izzy," Hanna heard Ma Etty say.

"Dang it!" A faucet ran.

"You have to get the food off them first!" A loud sigh. "Let me do it, Izzy. Go on. I know you're itching to ride."

Ma Etty was too nice to them. Izzy jogged back out of the kitchen.

"Come on," she said, grabbing Hanna by the arm and dragging her out ahead of the others, saying she wanted to talk in peace.

Talk? All they'd done was listen to the Lawnchairs together. For three hours. Okay, sure, they had laughed a lot about riding their horses and how cute Josh was. And sure, Izzy was a real joker, and most of the laughing was on Hanna's end as they pulled weeds to the thrumming of Noelle's guitar. But that didn't make them friends.

"You've already decided to do it, right?" Izzy prompted. "So why are you thinking about it?"

"What if he bucks? What if he rears?" Hanna rubbed her head. "What if I fall off?"

"So what? Wear a helmet. The worst that can happen is your butt gets a little bruised." Izzy shrugged as they approached the barn, and they opened the double doors together. "And Madison's helping you. What have you got to be afraid of?"

Everything, Hanna wanted to say. But for once, Izzy was right. She had Madison. This part was up to Hanna. No one else could ride Shy Guy for her.

And though she didn't want to admit it, she wanted to be the girl riding on his back with the wind flowing through her hair.

Eventually Fletch, Madison, Cade, Josh, and Rae Ann caught up to them in the barn.

"Change of plans, guys," said Fletch. "I know it's inconvenient, but I'm going to do a demonstration in the small corral today with my horse, Sawbones, so Hanna and Shy Guy can use the big arena." He glanced at Hanna. "That is, if you're still planning to ride today?"

Her throat had stopped working, and Hanna had to swallow three or four times before she could talk.

"Yes," she managed. "I am."

"Why does she get the whole practice arena?" asked Cade, puffing out his bottom lip.

Madison started, "Because—"

"Because she and Shy Guy need space, that's why!" Izzy glowered at Cade. He shrank back, even though she was probably a foot shorter than he was. "It's the first time he's been ridden by anybody in a long time, and the other horses make him nervous. Okay?"

"Okay, right, sorry!"

Madison and Fletch exchanged a look as Fletch led the kids out of the barn. Izzy was the last one to leave, and she flashed Hanna a thumbs-up on her way out.

"Before we do this," Madison said, getting a conspiratorial look in her eyes, "I want to give you something, Hanna."

She ducked into the tack room and rifled through a box of papers, pulling out a manila envelope. She handed it to Hanna and, like a kid who had worked hard on a homemade Christmas gift, said, "Open it!"

Hanna tore open the top and pulled out a heavy piece of metal. She turned it over. It was a gold nameplate with "Shy Guy" etched into it.

Her chest constricted. Madison's grin grew about as wide as her face.

"Will you do the honors of putting it on his stall?" she asked.

"Of course," Hanna whispered.

Together, they mounted the plate right in the middle of the door. It shimmered under the barn lights.

"Your patience and kindness brought Shy Guy to where he is now," said Madison. "So, are you ready to ride?" The look on her face was full of encouragement but underneath, a little trepidation.

Hanna nodded. "Ready as I'll ever be."

CHAPTER FIFTEEN

By the time Hanna was done with tacking up Shy Guy, he looked beautiful. Like a horse in a TV show.

He was ready to ride.

Madison led them out the back of the barn to the arena, where all the barrels and poles had been removed to leave an open, unthreatening space. Hanna swallowed and gripped the helmet in her hand tighter. She'd have to make sure that Madison put on the straps extra tight.

Just a bruised butt, she reminded herself. Walking beside Shy Guy, she was painfully aware of his massive size; of the muscles that rippled along his shoulders and his flanks; and of his heavy, sturdy hoofbeats.

But all that didn't frighten her anymore. When this thought made its way to the top, a surge of warm victory swept over her.

If Shy Guy did throw her, it wouldn't be on purpose. It would be out of fear or surprise or the multitude of other things that haunted an abused animal. She knew how unpredictable the ghost inside oneself could be.

Hanna put on the helmet, buckled the strap, and tightened it all on her own.

"Looks good," said Madison, rattling the helmet around on Hanna's head to test it. "Get on whenever you're ready. And please," she emphasized, concern seeping into her voice, "take your time. Stop if anything seems off."

Leading them over to a mounting block, Madison held the reins—though Shy Guy was suspicious of her at first—as Hanna picked up the stirrup in one hand.

"Here goes," Hanna said. She climbed up on the block and stuck her left foot in the stirrup. Shy Guy glanced back at her, ears perked, but he didn't move away.

Hanna reached for the horn and put all her weight in the stirrup. The saddle tilted slightly as she pushed up and swung her right leg over Shy Guy's back.

She settled back down, both feet in the stirrups. Shy Guy hadn't moved a muscle. Relief cascaded over Hanna.

"Wow," said Madison. "I can't believe it. We're really going to do this."

Frankly, Hanna couldn't believe it either. But the hard part was yet to come.

\\\

"Make sure you leave the reins a little slack," said Madison. "No, that's too much." She reached for the reins to adjust them, and Shy Guy's head swung away. Hanna let out a yelp as he jostled underneath her.

"Whoa," said Madison, backing away with her hands up. "Whoa, boy. Okay—you'll have to do all this on your own, Hanna. I can only give you instructions."

Hanna was still breathing hard from the shock of Shy Guy moving so suddenly. She tried to straighten her back and fix her posture to calm herself down. She would only frighten Shy Guy if she was afraid herself.

"Good," encouraged Madison. "Confidence will go a long way on a horse. Now ask him to walk."

Hanna lightly nudged Shy Guy with her heels,

and he started into a slow walk. Her breath caught in her throat.

He walked with a smooth, even gait, completely unlike Lacey's. Each step was controlled and fluid. It felt like floating.

She couldn't believe it. She was riding Shy Guy!

"Great job, Hanna," called Madison as they headed away. "Walk along the fence for a while, then try turning him."

When Hanna and Shy Guy had walked the entire circumference of the arena a few times, she pulled the reins across Shy Guy's neck to the left, to take him into the middle.

He balked for a second, as if he had forgotten what a bit in his mouth felt like. Hanna felt panic rise up in her, but she tamped it down and pulled the reins to the left again.

This time, his head followed. His whole body moved in the same direction, making him curve under her. He moved fluidly, like a snake, as she righted him again and they headed for the center of the arena. Madison stepped out of the way as they passed her.

Hanna had done it. She had asked him to turn, and he did. She was breathless with elation.

"Great!" Madison called after them, her voice laced with genuine surprise. "Looking really, really good. Keep on with the basic maneuvers."

Hanna and Shy Guy did another half of a lap, and then she turned him to the right. His right side was a little tougher than his left, but after a few tries, he turned and swept gracefully back into the center of the arena.

"Wow," said Madison. "He moves so smoothly. I wonder if he was trained in dressage."

"Dressage?" asked Hanna, as she and Shy Guy made another reverse figure eight.

"It's a high-level kind of English-style riding," she said. "It's mainly about the bond and communication between horse and rider, because they have to work together to do a series of complex movements. Requires a lot of skill. A good dressage horse is ultra responsive and graceful, so all the movements look effortless."

"Cool. So how do you know he was trained to do that?"

"I don't, but look at the way he responds to your cues," Madison said. "He's paying very close attention to you. So do you feel comfortable walking and doing basic turns?"

Hanna glanced down. She had forgotten she was even on a horse. Riding Shy Guy felt natural, easy. Like walking on her own two feet.

"I think so," she said.

"Great! Let's try taking him to a trot, then."

Hanna swallowed. She hated the bouncy trot and hoped she could keep it together.

Letting out some slack in the reins and leaning just the tiniest bit forward, she barely moved her feet before Shy Guy suddenly picked up his pace. Hanna held in a yelp, not wanting to frighten him.

But . . . his trot wasn't scary. And it certainly wasn't bumpy. Shy Guy simply slid into a longer walk, his legs reaching farther with each step— incredibly far, as if he were swimming through air.

"Holy cow," muttered Madison, watching them with golf ball–sized eyes as they passed her. "What even is that? An extended trot? How did you do that?"

"I don't know!" cried Hanna. They cruised, like a yacht on still water, around the arena. Whatever Shy Guy was doing, it didn't feel anything like Lacey's trot. Hanna's breaths grew shaky and uneven as she wondered what she'd done wrong.

But then a look of pure glee came over

Madison's face. "Here, Hanna—try this." She held out her hands. "Hold the reins tighter, and sit back a tiny bit."

"Tighter?" Hanna gathered up some of the slack in the reins and instantly, Shy Guy slowed down—but kept trotting. Hanna let out a squeak as she flew up on the saddle, her feet still tucked in the stirrups. She came back down, hard.

"Yowch!"

"Sorry!" called Madison. "Try matching his gait. Hanoverians are special-bred for smooth, predictable trots. When he goes up, let your natural bounce take you up too. Get in his rhythm."

Hanna had no idea what Madison meant, but as Shy Guy trotted around the arena, she tried to match her bounce to his. It took a few laps, but soon she wasn't hitting the saddle quite as hard—though she was sure she'd be bruised tomorrow.

Madison was shaking her head, and for a moment, Hanna thought she was disappointed or maybe angry. But when Madison looked up again, Hanna saw wonder on the trainer's face.

"I had no idea," she said, gesturing for the two of them to ride into the center of the arena. Hanna pulled the reins across Shy Guy's neck, and he immediately changed directions at a trot. "Now lean back to stop. You shouldn't even need to pull on the reins—sit back in your saddle and—"

Hanna adjusted her weight so she was sitting deep in the saddle, and Shy Guy ground to a complete halt. She was panting, and so was he.

The emotions came in a torrent. She had ridden Shy Guy. They had glided across the arena, together.

Before she could stop it, tears were rolling down her cheeks in big, messy streams.

Hanna collapsed forward on Shy Guy, wrapping her arms as far as they'd go around his huge neck. He turned his head slightly so she could reach his ears, and she rubbed behind them, not even caring about the saddle horn digging into her diaphragm. Her tears fell hot on his mane, disappearing in the silver-gray hairs.

"Oh, Hanna." Madison approached them slowly, but Shy Guy ignored her. Madison touched Hanna's knee reassuringly. "That was wild. I am so impressed. I can't believe how well you did. And you got him into an extended trot! I've never seen anything like that outside of dressage on TV. What did you do?"

"No idea," Hanna said. "He just . . . did it. I must have asked for it without knowing."

Carefully, Madison reached for Shy Guy's neck. He eyeballed her but didn't move away. With the gentlest of motions, Madison ran her hand through his long mane.

"What a horse," she said.

CHAPTER SIXTEEN

The rest of the day was a blur for Hanna. She couldn't stop smiling, and it was infectious. When the other kids heard the news, they clapped her on the back. At dinner, Mr. Bridle raised his water glass.

"Everyone," he said in his low, gravelly voice, "I'd like to propose a toast."

"A toast!" echoed Madison.

"To Hanna and Shy Guy. Congratulations on your first ride today."

Hanna felt her entire body turn red as everyone turned to look at her, also raising their glasses.

"To Hanna and Shy Guy," they repeated, clinking their glasses together. Rae Ann grinned at her.

Cade stopped studying his fingernails. Josh even brandished a rare smile. And everyone made a point of clinking Hanna's glass.

\\

In the girls' cabin late that night, after Madison had turned the lights out and gone into her room, Izzy whispered in the darkness.

"Hanna?" she said. "Are you awake?"

Before she replied, Hanna listened for Rae Ann's breathing. It was even and regular. She was asleep.

"Yeah?" Hanna finally answered.

"I . . ." She heard Izzy inhale sharply. "I'm sorry. I'm sorry I was mean to you. You're . . . you're actually pretty nice. And brave. And I kind of spied on you when you were riding today."

"You did?"

"You looked really cool out there. Way cooler than me. You . . . you're a natural."

Hanna swallowed hard.

"Thank you," she whispered into the dark.

"Whatever," said Izzy gruffly. "It's the truth."

\\

When Hanna and Shy Guy joined the other kids for their daily lesson a few days later, Madison warned them to keep some distance, just in case. But under a saddle, Shy Guy was confident. Sturdy.

Fearless.

Even when a barn cat got into the arena and frightened the other horses—especially Josh's horse, whom he hollered at in his Tennessee accent as it spooked and ran—Shy Guy stood his ground.

Hanna got him up to a canter that same day, and she couldn't hold back a shriek of excitement when they shot across the arena. Shy Guy's legs extended far out in front of him; it felt like they were flying.

"There it is again!" shouted Madison, grabbing Fletch's arm and pointing. "See? He can extend his canter too."

"Whoa." He took off his hat. "What in the name of . . .? Who trained him to do that?"

"Who knows," said Madison. Hanna blushed under their words, even though she knew it had nothing to do with her. It was all Shy Guy—a jewel hidden in plain sight.

When Hanna led Shy Guy through the barrel pattern, everyone cheered. Shy Guy strutted after that, like he knew he was a big shot.

Hanna could see she had a ham on her hands.

On Saturday, Madison and Fletch decided to let them skip chores and go on a trail ride into town for ice cream.

"Ice cream!" cried Izzy, flopping back on Fettucini as if he were a lawn chair. "I would kill for some cake batter ice cream. Or cookie dough."

"Hopefully you won't have to kill anyone," said Fletch, dropping his hat on Izzy's face as he rode past. "Because I'm pretty sure they have both."

"Woo-hoo!" Izzy turned to Hanna. "What's your favorite kind of ice cream? Do you think Shy Guy likes ice cream?"

Madison held up her hands. "I hate to break it to you, girls," she said, "but Hanna can't bring Shy Guy. If you want to come on the trail ride, Hanna, you'll have to ride Lacey."

"What?" asked Izzy. "But Shy Guy has been doing great in the arena."

Hanna understood, though. Trekking into a town full of cars and people would terrify Shy Guy. Could she handle him if something happened?

"I know, Izzy," said Madison. "It's not that I don't trust Hanna or Shy Guy. There are too many factors in play if we take him into town, and he's still so skittish . . ."

"From what I've seen, Maddie," Fletch offered, "Shy Guy is a different animal with someone in the saddle." Fletch leaned back, leaving Sawbones's reins hanging over the horse's freckled neck. "He's not faint of heart, and he listens to Hanna without question. Remember when Shy Guy didn't even blink at that cat?"

"That's true," Madison allowed.

"He's the kind of horse that respects confidence." Fletch looked hard at Hanna. "Whenever you tell him what to do and he listens, he's passing the authority to you. He's putting his life in your hands. He believes in you so much, Hanna. You could blindfold a horse like Shy Guy and he'd do whatever you told him, trusting you not to walk him over a cliff."

"I'd never do that," gasped Hanna.

"Of course not. But you see my point?"

"Yeah."

"You're in control. You decide what goes. Whether he spooks on this ride is up to you." Fletch arched one eyebrow and leaned forward. "Do you feel confident, Hanna?"

Was that all it took? Confidence?

"Yes," she said, her own certainty surprising

her. But she was—she had total confidence in Shy Guy now. She could feel the connection between them, the trust they'd forged, every time she sat in the saddle.

Fletch threw a grin at Madison and shrugged his shoulders, like he'd proven his point. Madison made an annoyed, thinking noise.

"Okay," she said eventually. "Fine. If you think you can handle it, Hanna, Shy Guy can come with us."

"I know I can," Hanna said. "And so can he."

"Awesome!" Izzy whooped. Every horse startled at the noise except Shy Guy. Madison just shook her head.

Getting out on the road with Shy Guy was a different tin of sardines from riding in the arena. But Hanna had trusted in Shy Guy so far, and look how far they'd come.

Madison, riding her spotted horse, and Fletch, with his freckly red roan, led the group off Bridlemile Road and onto a special trail that crisscrossed the patchwork of farms and ranches of Quartz Creek, far from the highway. At its opposite end, the trail spilled out right onto downtown Main Street.

"Everyone rode horses here at one time," said Fletch, pointing out the tie poles scattered all over town. "You'd ride up to the General Store, tie up your horse, and do your grocery shopping."

People waved at them as they walked down the street. Cars slowed down and gave them a wide berth. Shy Guy walked with his head high, unperturbed by vehicles or people or pavement. As they arrived at the ice-cream shop and tied up their horses, Fletch winked at Hanna and said, "Told you."

Hanna and Fletch stayed with the horses while the others went in for ice cream. Izzy promised to get Hanna's order for her.

All the Quartz Creek Ranchers ate together outside. Rae Ann somehow managed to get ice cream on Cade's face, and Izzy practically inhaled hers.

"How on earth did you do that so fast?" asked Josh.

"I don't get brain freezes." To demonstrate, Izzy took Madison's leftover ice cream and sank her teeth directly into it. Everyone winced.

Hanna wasn't watching. She studied Shy Guy, who simply stood tied by the other horses, lazily swatting flies with his tail. As she finished her ice cream, she felt buoyant, like a balloon rising into the sky.

\\

During dinner that night, a car came grumbling down the driveway. Conversation at the table halted.

"Are we expecting anyone, honey?" Mr. Bridle asked his wife.

Ma Etty shook her head. "No—not that I know of. But it could be the Goodsteins."

Mr. Bridle rose to his feet and peered out the dining room window. "Not Jim's truck," he said.

No one spoke as the car pulled into the parking lot. Mr. Bridle and Ma Etty got up to answer it. The air buzzed with anticipation. No one had come to the ranch this late before, especially not unannounced.

After a long, loaded silence, a knock came at the door. In the other room, the door creaked as it opened.

"Hello," Hanna heard Mr. Bridle say. "What can I help you with at this hour?" He stressed *this hour*, as if to impress upon the visitor that the late visit was unwelcome.

Heeled shoes clicked on the wood floors. Izzy got out of her chair and scurried to look.

"Izzy!" Madison hissed, but Izzy ignored her, peering into the living room.

"My name is Elena Baxter," boomed a woman's voice, sharp and steely. "This is my husband, John Curry."

Josh followed Izzy, peering over her short head.

"Josh!" Fletch tried this time, but the kids couldn't be stopped. Eventually, Rae Ann and Cade got up too, and soon Madison and Fletch couldn't help their curiosity either. Hanna was the last to join them in the doorway, openly staring at the couple who had arrived on the ranch's doorstep.

The woman stood as tall as Mr. Bridle and thin, dressed in a white, billowy blouse and dark-washed jeans. Everything on her gleamed, from her flashy earrings to her faux crocodile skin boots. Her husband, a stout, older man with a deeply receded hairline, huddled behind her.

"What can we help you with this evening, Ms. Baxter?" asked Ma Etty, her politeness almost sounding genuine.

"We're here about our horse."

"Pardon me, but what horse?" asked Ma Etty. "I

don't know you, and neither do I know your animals."

"Yes, you do. You have my horse, Star Dancer."

Ma Etty shook her head. "Sorry," she said. "There's no horse here named Star Dancer."

Elena took another step into the house. Something about her made Hanna shrink back from the doorway. Her face was all sharp angles, no dimples—strange for someone her age. It was like she had never smiled in her life. "I think you do. In fact, I know you do."

"I'm sorry," Ma Etty repeated, taking a matching step closer. Mr. Bridle stayed put, as if his wife was more fit to handle this than he was. "We really don't have your horse."

"But I saw one of your girls riding him around town today. The big gray Hanoverian—that's our Star Dancer!" Elena Baxter clasped her hands in front of her. "I've been looking for him for so long."

There was only one big gray Hanoverian at Quartz Creek Ranch. Hanna's heart dropped. The woman had to be mistaken.

"I think you've made an error," said Ma Etty evenly. "That horse—*Shy Guy*—was abandoned on our property, and we took him in."

"No, no," said Elena. "I think you're the one

who's made a mistake. I went on a short vacation to Europe. When I returned, my beloved Star Dancer was gone. He must have escaped, or—"

"Then that was a different horse. When we took in Shy Guy, no horses had been reported missing to the sheriff."

The two women stared each other down, despite the immense height gap between them.

"Do you know who I am?" said Elena. "My mother was an Olympic dressage rider. She was known all over the world."

"No, I don't know you," said Ma Etty. "Or your mother. It's not going to change my opinion on the horse."

"I insist you return him to me. This is theft."

Hanna only felt total and complete horror.

"How dare you—!" Ma Etty stopped mid-sentence and took a deep, calming breath. "Ms. Baxter," she began again, squaring her shoulders. "Please refrain from making such unfounded accusations until you can prove it—with paperwork."

"If that's what it takes," Elena said. "You'll be seeing me again very soon. I promise you." Elena turned, grabbed her husband's hand, and yanked him out the still-open door.

Outside, the engine roared to life. The car veered at full speed back onto Bridlemile Road, the red taillights flickering in the window of the main room as the couple sped away.

Hanna burned from head to toe. She couldn't tell if it was fear or anger—all she knew was that she really wanted to grab one of that woman's crocodile skin boots and hit her with it.

"You okay?" Izzy asked her.

Hanna shook her head, unable to speak. Izzy hugged Hanna with one arm, frizzy curls brushing her face.

"Everyone back into the dining room," said Ma Etty. "That woman has a case of mistaken identity. I'm sure we've seen the last of her."

But a knot of dread had settled in Hanna's stomach. She didn't think Elena Baxter would go away that easily.

CHAPTER SEVENTEEN

A dreary silence settled over the ranch the next day. Clouds had rolled in overnight, and in the morning, they turned dark and angry. Riding lessons were canceled because of a storm warning. Ma Etty didn't even have the spirit to assign jobs that day, so when it started raining and thundering in the afternoon, she called everyone inside for board games and a movie instead.

It felt like a rainy Saturday when Hanna was little—when her dad didn't travel so much and her mom wasn't so anxious.

Paul came to the house as soon as he heard about the strange visitors. He and Ma Etty disappeared down the hall, talking in hushed voices.

Izzy got up and gestured at Hanna to follow her.

"What?" Hanna whispered.

"Come on. I want to hear." They made off like they were going to use the bathroom but stood outside the office door instead, listening to the conversation inside.

"Baxter, huh?" Paul was saying. "Yeah. I do know her. They moved here when I was in high school, from somewhere east. I never heard why, but I did meet her mother once—Juliet Baxter. She went to the Olympic Games in '68, I think. Came back with a bronze. Scary lady too, just like her daughter. I heard she left Elena a bunch of money, but she's blown most of it on having horses shipped over from Europe."

"Horses, plural?" asked Ma Etty.

"Yeah—gets a new one every few years. It's a big event when one of those fancy trailers rolls into town, you know? But I don't think she keeps them long."

"Probably because she ruins them, just like she did Shy Guy."

"I reckon you're right, Etty." He sighed. "She's going to come back with papers, you know. No way that big horse isn't hers. And she's gonna want him back, now that Hanna's fixed him up."

"I know," Ma Etty said with a sad sigh. "I know, Paul."

Izzy noticed Hanna's tears before she did. "It'll be fine," she whispered. "I'm sure of it."

\\

The knock came around 5 p.m. Ma Etty rose from her spot on the floor playing the banker in Monopoly and went into the entryway. Everyone stood up to see what was happening, but Madison ushered them into the dining room to start setting the table. Izzy and Hanna lingered in the hallway, and no one hassled them.

When Ma Etty opened the door, Elena stood on the other side dressed in jeans and riding boots, her hair pulled back in a tight, high bun. Beside her stood a tiny older woman with glasses.

Ma Etty did not invite them in. "Hello again."

"This is my lawyer, Ms. Marcelle," Elena said. The lawyer did not extend her hand but, instead, held out a manila envelope.

"What's this?" asked Ma Etty.

"An injunction. To release my horse." Elena gestured to the gleaming white trailer sitting in the parking lot. "I trust you'll cooperate in bringing Star Dancer out so I can load him into my trailer, and I won't report to the sheriff that one of your hoodlums stole him."

Ma Etty's hands balled into fists. "They are not—" She stopped herself; took a long, calming breath; and took the envelope.

Hanna squeezed her eyes shut and then opened them again, hoping this was all a nightmare. Her pulse hammered as Ma Etty undid the clasp on the envelope and pulled out a piece of paper. She read for a short time, and Hanna wished she could see her face.

Then Ma Etty's hands fell to her sides.

"He's out in the barn," she said, her voice painfully quiet. "Will, can you—?"

Mr. Bridle set his hands on her shoulders and steered her back into the house. "Give us some time," he told the lawyer, not looking at Elena, and closed the door in their faces.

When Ma Etty turned around, her eyes met Hanna's.

"Hanna," she said, gesturing at her to come over.

She drew Hanna in for an embrace. "I think you know what this means."

Hanna could only nod, her whole face hot and swollen with tears. They hadn't broken through yet, but her nose felt like a volcano ready to burst. She didn't believe it. That woman really was Shy Guy's owner. His old, abusive owner. He'd tried to escape her once, but she'd found him again.

"I'm so sorry," Ma Etty said. "We'll do whatever we can to fight this, believe me. But for now, we have to let her take Shy Guy. Okay?"

Hanna nodded slowly. It would be temporary until they could get a scary-looking lawyer too. Right? Isn't that how these things worked?

"But . . . Hanna." Ma Etty looked her in the eye. "I can't promise anything. If that Baxter woman is Shy Guy's owner, if those papers are real, then we have to give him up. He's not ours."

"But she hurt him!" cried Hanna, pushing Ma Etty away. "She hit him so much he ran away from her! That woman is evil. She *can't* have him back."

"Hanna's right," said Izzy. "Elena Baxter is abusive. She'll send Shy Guy back to the way he was before."

"We can't prove that she's ever done anything

wrong," said Madison, who had followed Izzy. "There's no evidence. Not anymore."

Another knock came at the door. Mr. Bridle's face turned beet red.

"We're coming!" he roared, and everyone stood stock-still. He took a few deep breaths and then wiped his forehead under his hat and replaced it on his head. "Can't stand those impatient city people."

"There's nothing we can do right now," said Ma Etty in her calmest voice. "But we'll talk to the sheriff later and find out what options we have. That's all we've got right now." She turned away from Hanna. "Paul, Will—it's time to go out to the barn."

"I need to say good-bye!" cried Hanna, lunging after Paul and Mr. Bridle as they headed for the door. She couldn't let them take Shy Guy without getting to see him one last time. The tears that had threatened behind her eyes finally burst free, and they burned as they ran down her cheeks.

"You can go with them," assured Ma Etty. "But don't help them get Shy Guy into the trailer. We'll see then what this Baxter woman is about."

CHAPTER EIGHTEEN

Outside, rain pelted the ground in torrents and the sky was so muddy black that it was impossible to tell whether the sun had gone down. Even in the parka Ma Etty had put over her, Hanna shivered as she walked between Paul and Mr. Bridle out to the barn. The black shale roofing shuddered in a gust of wind.

When Mr. Bridle opened the barn door, a gale ripped it out of his hand and slammed it against the barn wall. The horses neighed in their stalls. As he reached to get the door back under control, Hanna and Paul rushed into the barn. Mr. Bridle followed them in, latching it closed behind them.

Inside, Hanna pulled down the hood of her

parka. The barn was quiet save for the gentle shaking of the walls in the wind and the occasional whinny of a horse. The air was electrified.

When Paul went to take the green halter off Shy Guy's stall, Hanna stopped him.

"Use a different one."

He gave her an odd look but grabbed a junky old one from the tack room anyway. Shy Guy's shiny new nameplate flickered as Paul opened the stall door.

When Shy Guy saw the strange man, he retreated a few steps back into the darkness, his eyes bulging and worried.

"Hanna," said Mr. Bridle, "can you help us get him out?"

Anger shot through her—not at Mr. Bridle but at Elena Baxter. At the whole world. Why should she help that horrible woman take Shy Guy away? She'd be complicit in betraying him.

"No," Hanna said, stepping back from the stall. "If she wants him, she can get him herself."

Mr. Bridle looked at her long and hard and then nodded. Instead, Paul strode into the stall with the halter hanging over one arm and reached to put the lead rope around Shy Guy's neck.

Shy Guy pressed himself against the far back wall, but Paul wouldn't give up. Despite Shy Guy tossing his head, Paul managed to get the halter over his nose and buckle it behind his ears.

"Shh," said Paul, trying to calm him. "It's only rain." He tugged on the lead rope toward the open stall door, but Shy Guy wouldn't budge. He'd put his ears so far back they were nearly flush with his head, and his frightened eyes flicked from Hanna to Paul and back to Hanna again.

He was terrified. Not of the rain—but of this strange person, of the tension and fear buzzing in the air. It felt like he could even see the tears on Hanna's soaked face and knew something bad was coming.

"Come on, boy," called Mr. Bridle, grabbing a bucket of grain. But even shaking the pail didn't help, and Shy Guy tried to make himself as small as possible in the back of the stall.

Hanna's heart crumbled. He was so frightened, and refusing to help only made it worse. Elena Baxter was going to take him away, no matter what.

She owed it to him to make it less painful if she could.

"Here," Hanna said, walking into the stall and taking the lead rope from Paul. Shy Guy's ears immediately pricked forward, and his silver head reached out toward her from the shadows. Hanna lifted her hand, running her fingers over his velvety nose. He took a step toward her and weaved his head through her arms.

Shy Guy's nostrils flared as she brushed his face. He could smell that she was afraid. He nudged her chest.

"I'm sorry," Hanna whispered, pushing his forelock out of his eyes. He blinked gentle brown eyes. "I told you I'd protect you," she murmured in his ear. "But I can't. It's only temporary, though. I'll get you back. We'll get you back, Shy Guy. I promise."

He snuffled her hand, hoping for a treat. She still had some stashed in her pocket, so she produced one, and he lipped her hand before eating it up. She was never afraid he'd bite her. He had the gentlest soul of any creature she'd ever met.

Elena Baxter didn't deserve him.

Shy Guy waited obediently as Hanna left the stall, then came out after her, turning around so she could close the door behind them.

Mr. Bridle had propped the barn door open, and a cold, wet wind stole inside, shuffling a paper tacked to the wall. Shy Guy's ears flicked back and forth, but not anxiously. He had no idea who was waiting to take him away.

Hanna felt like a traitor.

After ushering them outside, Mr. Bridle shut the barn door. The sudden noise startled Shy Guy, but at Hanna's side, he didn't spook.

"You did well with him," Mr. Bridle said.

"I didn't do anything," said Hanna. "It was all Shy Guy." She was glad for the rain because it hid the fresh tears that rushed down her face.

Paul pointed toward the gleaming white trailer in the parking lot. "Let's go."

Together, Paul, Mr. Bridle, Hanna, and Shy Guy crossed the little bridge over the creek onto the gravel road, which now ran black with mud. The closer they got to the white trailer, the more Hanna wanted to turn around and run away with Shy Guy, off into the woods, where there were no Elena Baxters who could hurt him.

They stepped into the parking lot and Hanna swallowed. Elena approached in a hooded, silvery raincoat, so not a hair on her head was wet. Hanna found an ounce of pleasure in the big splotch of mud staining the hem.

Elena extended one hand for the lead rope. Behind her, her husband lifted the latch on the back of the trailer and lowered the ramp.

"I know what you did to him," Hanna growled.

"I don't know what you mean." Elena shook her hand, emphasizing that she wanted the lead rope, and Shy Guy shied away—whether from the sudden movement or because he recognized Elena, Hanna didn't know. "Now, please, dear, hand him over."

"I know how you hurt him," said Hanna, clutching the lead rope tightly. "And even if we can't prove it—"

"Hanna," Mr. Bridle told her. "Now is not the time."

But she didn't let go. She pressed her hand to Shy Guy's cheek, and he watched her, eyes frightened.

"Yes," Elena echoed, "now isn't the time. The lawyers can fight it out later if you insist on it. Anyway," she leaned forward and patted Hanna's head, "what good would a horse like Star Dancer do an inexperienced child like you? He's been trained in Germany by the best in the business. He's a Grand Prix competitor. Who knows what damage your novice riding has already done to him?"

"Me? Damage him?" cried Hanna. "You—!"

Reaching out a third time for the lead rope, Elena plucked it right out of Hanna's hands. Hanna grappled to get it back, but Mr. Bridle took her by the shoulders and drew her away.

"No!" Hanna shouted, reaching for the lead rope, for Shy Guy, for anything. She couldn't let him go. She wouldn't. "No! Shy Guy!" Shy Guy neighed and yanked his head away from Elena, but her grip was iron strong. His eyes widened and his nostrils flared as she tugged him toward the open trailer door.

"Please control your hoodlum," Elena snapped at Mr. Bridle as Shy Guy pulled again. "She's frightening him. Whoa, boy. Whoa!"

"It's you who's frightening him!" Hanna couldn't control the sobs that tumbled out of her as Mr. Bridle led her away to where Ma Etty stood on the front step.

"We can't do anything right now," Ma Etty said, wrapping her arm around Hanna's shaking shoulders and positioning an umbrella over them both. "But I promise, tomorrow, we'll do whatever we can."

"You can't let her take him!" Hanna cried, but she had stopped struggling.

"I'm so sorry," was all Ma Etty could say.

When Shy Guy continued backing away from

the trailer, Elena's husband emerged with a whip. The whip cracked and Shy Guy reared up, hooves clawing the air. But Elena wasn't frightened. She simply yanked on the lead rope and yelled, "Get in!"

"Idiot woman," growled Mr. Bridle. "Didn't even open the windows inside. Who'd walk into a dark box?"

"He's so scared," Hanna said in a tiny voice.

Elena snatched the whip from her husband and, holding the lead rope in one hand and the whip in the other, smacked Shy Guy across the rump.

Lightning shot down from the sky, turning the black clouds bright white.

Shy Guy's ears flattened against his head, and he let out a horrible neigh. The third time the whip snapped, he jolted forward. Ears flattened to his skull and tail thrashing wildly, he finally hopped into the trailer.

"What a good horse," murmured Paul, as the trailer ramp went back up and Elena latched it closed behind him. She returned to the truck and climbed inside.

Her husband went around to the passenger side door, then paused, and closed it again. He approached Hanna and Ma Etty.

"You have to understand," he said quickly. "He's the last one. He's all she's got. She's not trying to hurt you, little girl. She just wants her horse back."

"I want him back too," said Hanna.

"Just, please." His lower lip trembled. "Please, don't blame her. Elena knows no other way."

A head leaned out the truck's window. "Come on, John!" Elena shouted. The squat man just shook his head and returned to the truck, getting in after her.

The truck's engine roared to life and the vehicle started backing out. When the headlights blazed on and it started to drive away, Hanna suddenly shrieked and ran after it.

This was her last chance.

"Shy Guy!" she cried. Everything they'd been through, everything they'd done together—it was all for nothing. Elena was going to ruin him all over again, and she couldn't save him, not this time. "Shy Guy!"

But it didn't matter. The truck roared off down Bridlemile Road, heedless of her. The last thing Hanna saw was Shy Guy's gray tail blowing in the wind as it vanished into the night.

CHAPTER NINETEEN

"There must be something we can do." It was the third time Ma Etty had said that since she got on the phone with the sheriff earlier that morning, and Hanna's heart sank even further. "Can we file a counter injunction?"

There was noise on the other end of the line, and Ma Etty's lips pursed into a deep scowl. Hanna had never seen this side of her before. She and Izzy leaned forward in their chairs. For the first time, the Bridles had allowed ranch kids into their small office in the back of the house (the one with a paper sign reading *Internal Affairs* taped on it). But to Hanna, it wasn't a privilege. She couldn't think of anything but getting Shy Guy out of that awful woman's clutches.

"Well, I don't know these things, Doug," Ma Etty shot back at the phone. "Fine. I need to make a few phone calls, but I'll be calling you back." She hung up and turned to Mr. Bridle. "Will, I need you to call Ron."

When Mr. Bridle took the phone, Ma Etty explained that Ron was their lawyer, and he should be able to help. But a few minutes later, Mr. Bridle returned, his face lined with defeat.

"Ron says there's nothing he can do. Elena Baxter has purchase papers for Shy Guy—*Star Dancer*—and he fits the bill, markings and all. He's all hers."

That was it. They were out of options.

Hanna desperately needed some air. She walked out of the office and left the house. Izzy followed, not saying anything. But it helped just knowing she was there.

The wind and the rain had died down since the previous night, leaving the sky overcast and gray. The downpour had filled the creek to overflowing, leaving the driveway and pasture wet and muddy.

It was past time for riding lessons to start.

"Hey, girls," Madison called to them, as if on cue. She walked over, swinging a halter and forcing a smile. "Ready to join the rest of us for lessons?"

Hanna shrugged, and they followed Madison back to the arena, where the other kids were working with Fletch. Rae Ann trotted over when she saw them.

"How did it go?" she asked. "Is Shy Guy coming back?"

Josh, Cade, and Fletch joined her. Hanna was so shaken that she realized she couldn't speak, but luckily, Izzy stepped in.

"Elena has papers proving she owns Shy Guy," she said. Her eyebrows lowered dangerously. "She even told the sheriff that she thinks one of us stole him."

"What?" cried Rae Ann. "How could she?"

"She has no proof," growled Josh.

Cade sat back abruptly. "That's a crock."

Hanna nodded, helpless. "There's nothing we can do," she said.

Everyone was silent, not sure what to say.

"Tomorrow's another day," said Fletch eventually. "I'm sure the Bridles will figure something out. Come on, everyone. We've got a lesson to finish."

After lights went out that night and Madison closed her door, Izzy didn't even wait for Rae Ann to fall asleep before whispering to Hanna in the dark.

"We have to get him back," Izzy said.

"How?" asked Hanna wearily. "What can we possibly do?"

"What if we broke in and stole him? Maybe camouflaged him or hid him somewhere on the property where Elena couldn't find him?"

"And what, get arrested? She'll know we took him. And so will Paul when he finds him, not to mention the sheriff . . ." Hanna sighed. "Sorry, Izz. I don't mean to shoot you down. I've just thought of all this before."

"We understand," said Rae Ann. "You love him. Like I love my Sadie."

Hanna's chest ached. She felt a lot more strongly about her horse than about a cat. "Yeah," she said. "Like Sadie."

Rae Ann plowed on. "We should ask the boys. I bet they have some good ideas. Josh is really smart."

"Together we can think of something," said Izzy, her voice steady and sure. "I know we can. We have to, for Shy Guy's sake."

Hanna didn't want to talk anymore. She was

tired and her head hurt and her mind swam with images of Elena hitting Shy Guy—sometimes with the whip, sometimes with her bare hands. Every time Hanna heard the same cracking sound.

She wanted to fall asleep and never wake up again.

"Let me know when you've all come up with your great idea," Hanna said, curling into a ball on her bed.

"Don't worry," Izzy replied, without an ounce of doubt in her voice. "We will."

\\

The next day, Madison asked Hanna to ride Lacey during the lesson, and she agreed without thinking about it. It was all the same to her.

In the ring, Lacey was . . . well, a horse. She did everything that Hanna knew how to ask for—and she did it completely placidly, without any of Shy Guy's smooth grace or spirit. Hanna and Lacey were both robots, doing what they were told.

Lacey was a fine horse.

Hanna didn't really care.

"Good work, Hanna!" Fletch called from the edge of the arena as she completed the keyhole.

"Lacey's really responding to you."

"Thanks," she muttered and walked to the back of the line behind Josh.

"Hey," he said. "Since we have free time this afternoon, you want to play bean bag toss?"

"Isn't it a little muddy still?"

He glanced around at the trenches their horses had carved in the arena, thanks to the rain.

"I guess so. Well, maybe Monopoly? You owe me a rematch."

Hanna shrugged. "Sure."

Josh's slight smile faded. "I'm really sorry about Shy Guy. That was such . . ." He sounded like he was about to say a curse word, but Madison was standing right near them, so he coughed and went on. "I can't believe the nerve of that lady."

"Yeah," she said as Cade finished his turn. "Nothing I can do now but try and forget."

He furrowed his eyebrows. "Forget?"

"Josh!" Fletch was trying to get his attention. "Your turn."

The rest of training, Hanna didn't speak to anyone. As they were putting the horses away, Cade came over to help her close up Lacey's stall.

"Hey, Hanna," he said. "I know you're really sad

right now. We all are. But I hope you know . . . we're here for you. And I hope you don't actually forget about Shy Guy and what you did for him. I'm sure he won't forget you."

Hanna's throat tightened. "Thanks, Cade." She bowed her head. "You're right. I could never forget him."

"Remember the good things. And, well," he looked around and lowered his voice, "if you do come up with a plan to get him back, I'll be the first to help you. I have over four hundred hours of experience as a tactician in my Team Strike Ops guild! Undercover missions are my specialty."

Hanna cast an annoyed glance at Izzy, who gave a sheepish shrug.

"Seriously," Cade said. "Josh and I are standing by, ready to assist."

The dedication in his voice made Hanna pause. He sounded so confident that it could be done, that there was no reason to give up hope.

She started to wonder if maybe there was something they could do.

The day Hanna realized she'd been at Quartz Creek Ranch for more than a month was the day she realized she hadn't once missed home. Or her mom, for that matter. Mom was probably itching to call, but she knew the ranch rules: no visits, no letters, and no phone calls. One of the few things Hanna could appreciate.

It had been a week since that rainy night, and her thoughts were still consumed with Shy Guy— with the feeling of total freedom she'd felt as they flew together across the arena, the wind whipping her hair back.

What was he doing now? How was Elena treating him? Each day Hanna felt worse, rather than better. She thought, unfortunately, it was probably the same for Shy Guy.

She had to save him, but she didn't know how.

One evening during free time, Hanna took Izzy's elbow and pulled her aside.

"I don't have an idea yet," she whispered, "but I want to see if the Internet can help us."

"What do you want to find?" Izzy asked, her brown eyes lighting up with hope and curiosity.

"Where Elena Baxter lives. What she does. Anything we could use against her."

Izzy's smile was devilish. "Yeah!"

Hanna asked Ma Etty if they could use an hour of their free time to look something up online.

"Sure," she said, not even putting down her newspaper. "I'll come get you when your time's up."

Once they had the computer to themselves, they looked up Elena Baxter's name, hoping they could find her house, anything about her that might be helpful.

But it wasn't Elena's name that brought up search results—it was her mother, the Olympic athlete, who kept appearing.

Honoring Our Coloradan Olympians.

Dressage Hall of Fame: Great Olympic Goofs that Cost a Medal.

Olympian Juliet Baxter's Legacy Lives On—Daughter Announces Entry Into Olympic Competition.

"That's her," said Izzy, pointing at the screen. It was dated over five years ago. Hanna clicked on it, but after scanning the article, didn't find any useful information about Elena besides a heavily doctored photo of her face.

"She looks way too old to be going to the Olympics," said Izzy.

"Ugh," said Hanna. She started writing an angry comment at the bottom of the article. "I hate her."

"Don't." Izzy deleted the text before Hanna could post it and navigated back to the search screen. "Come on. Let's look for something else."

The next result was for Elena's dubious-looking real estate business. It listed an office address and phone number but nothing else. Hanna closed the window in frustration.

Even if they had found Elena's address, what would they have done with it? Stolen Shy Guy for real, only to end up in jail? It was a pointless exercise, Hanna realized, and got up halfway through their hour. She went out to the garden to pull weeds instead.

Izzy came out to find Hanna later and crouched in the dirt next to her.

"You're pulling weeds. With your only free time." She said it as a statement, rather than a question.

"So?"

"So that's pathetic."

"Thanks," muttered Hanna. "That makes me feel so much better about it."

Izzy's mouth opened to make a retort, but they

were interrupted by Paul calling their names. Izzy shot up, her crush on the handsome blond ranch manager blatantly obvious. Hanna thought it was kind of gross.

"He's, like, thirty," Hanna had said.

"So?" Izzy shrugged. "He looks exactly like young Brad Pitt. Swoon!" Hanna had to agree about the Brad Pitt thing.

"Hey, girls!" Paul greeted, leaning up against his truck. He gestured with his thumb to the cab. "I need some helpers to come with me and pick up feed. I know you're on free time, but if you come with me, we can get subs at the sub shop."

Neither of them had eaten out since getting to the ranch, so Izzy jumped to her feet.

"Subs and ice cream, and you've got a deal."

"Done," said Paul, and opened the back doors of his four-door truck. The girls hopped in, and they roared off to Quartz Creek.

CHAPTER TWENTY

At the feed store, Paul got sidetracked by a work boot sale, so Izzy said, "Let's go look around out back while Brad gets his shop on."

Outside, the feed store lot was piled high with stacks of hay bales, bags of grain, and rusted farm equipment. "Check it out!" Izzy pointed past tractors with no tires and a dismembered Caterpillar claw to a graveyard full of old cars.

Before Hanna could stop her, Izzy clambered over the equipment in a way that Hanna was sure Paul would not approve of and vanished.

"Izzy!" Hanna called after her, but she was gone. With a sigh, Hanna followed.

On the other side of the junk pile, Izzy roamed through rows of old, broken-down cars, *oooh*-ing and *ahh*-ing. "Look at this, a '51 Mustang!"

"You like junky cars?" asked Hanna.

Izzy shrugged. "My dad collects scrap cars like this, and I used to help him fix them up." She laughed. "My mom hates it, though. Takes up a lot of space."

"You don't help him anymore?" Hanna asked.

Izzy paused next to an old Chevy truck. She patted the domed hood. "No. Not since I started getting in trouble at school."

She stopped and gave Hanna a calculating look, like she was trying to decide whether to trust her with more. After a moment, Izzy went on.

"My parents figured they needed to spend more time with me. And that was what I wanted! But they treated me so differently. When my mom and I used to garden together, we'd listen to music and she'd tell me about the different instruments and styles. But after things at school got bad, she'd make me stay inside to do my homework and look over my shoulder the whole time. Dad used to ask me to help him with the cars, but now he lectures me about why school's important or why fighting won't get me anywhere. Instead of looking at me like his helpful assistant, he looks at me like I'm the thing that needs fixing. And maybe I am."

She stopped talking and walked around the old Chevy, opening the rusty door. She climbed inside and leaned back in the seat.

"Careful," said Hanna. "There could be mice."

Izzy shrugged. "I'm not scared of mice. But sounds like you are."

"I'm not!"

"You're scared of horses," said Izzy. "And I don't see how horses could possibly be scarier than mice. I mean, those long, scaly tails! And they're diseased."

"Are you kidding?" said Hanna, climbing in the passenger seat to prove her wrong. "Horses are totally scarier. They're huge, for starters."

"Of course."

"And you never know what they're going to do. They could kick you, and *bam*, you're done."

Izzy narrowed her eyes. "Has a horse ever tried to kick you?"

"Well, no."

"Then what's your deal? You know, way back when, I heard Madison say you liked horses."

Hanna rolled her eyes. "When I was, like, seven!

My mom told her that because I used to collect little toy horses."

"So what's the difference?"

"Well, there's a big difference. One's a toy. One's big enough to kill you."

Izzy narrowed her eyes and leaned over the middle seat toward her. Hanna leaned away. "What happened?" Izzy asked. "Did something happen?"

"No," Hanna said automatically.

"Come on, Hanna. Tell me. I told you my secret. What made you so freaked out about horses?"

Hanna swallowed. Izzy was right. Fair trade.

"Mom took me to the county fair," Hanna said. "I was seven. I'd been collecting toy horses forever, so when we got to the pony ride, she insisted I do it." Remembering it, her pulse jumped. "But the horses were so much bigger in real life, and I didn't want to ride. But Mom made me. As soon as I got on that pony, I started crying."

"Did it throw you or something?"

Hanna slowly shook her head. "No. We walked around in a circle for twenty minutes. That's it. But it felt like forever, Izz. I wanted down more than anything, but Mom kept saying, 'Hanna! You love horses. Come on, I bought this ride for you. Why can't you have fun? Why are you making a scene?' And I kept crying and crying, but I didn't want my mom to get mad at me, so I stayed on the horse."

Izzy let out a breath. "And I thought my mom was a piece of work."

"Sometimes I think she wishes I was somebody else. Like, wishes she'd had a different daughter."

"I feel that," Izzy said, sighing. "Me too. I still don't understand what that has to do with stealing or how you, of all people, ended up at QCR. You're scared of ponies walking around in a circle. Nice white girls like you don't get sent to rehab camp just for stealing a candy bar."

Hanna didn't know how to put it into words.

"I guess I wanted to stick it to her," Hanna said finally. "Show her I could be horrible too. Make her miss the old me."

"Still don't get what that has to do with stealing," said Izzy.

"She's always getting on my case about everything!" The venom in Hanna's voice surprised even her. "If I get an A instead of an A-plus, she flips out. She says my friends talk too loud or I eat too fast or my piano should be better, but I've only been playing for a year! I practiced every single day. But nothing is ever enough for her." Something dark crept into her tone. "So I decided to do something she'd hate."

Izzy looked genuinely worried.

"At first, I took stuff right where Mom could see. Then, when I got away with it, whenever I could. But . . . it was impossible to stop." She collapsed back in the ripped leather seat. "She finally figured it out when she cleaned under my bed and found everything."

"Everything?" prompted Izzy.

"Candy, lipstick, an iPod . . ."

"Dude," said Izzy, whistling. "You were hard-core."

"I guess." That unsettled Hanna. She didn't want to be good at stealing. After a moment of quiet, she said, "We should go back, in case Brad Pitt is looking for us."

"Good call," said Izzy.

Together they climbed out of the car and shut the doors, leaving their puddle of spilled secrets behind. But when Hanna glanced past the feed store lot fence, she spotted a familiar gray horse trotting past.

Her entire body went white-hot.

"Izzy," she hissed, pointing. "Look, Shy Guy!"

Elena Baxter, dressed in high leather riding boots, rode Shy Guy past on a little black English saddle. He performed a long, canter-like gait along the perimeter of the fence. He was lathered in sweat. Elena hit him with the whip every time he slowed down or missed a step, and Shy Guy pressed his ears back but obeyed nevertheless.

"Come on," she growled. "Stop messing up that lead change!" Angrily she yanked on the reins, and Shy Guy stumbled over his own feet.

Hanna's face burned. She wanted to strangle that woman. Shy Guy worked and worked, and Elena Baxter didn't appreciate an ounce of it. Hanna had never hated someone so much in her life.

As if he knew Hanna was nearby, Shy Guy ground to a halt. Elena tried to make him trot, but he wouldn't budge. His ears flicked forward, searching for something.

"Come on, you dumb horse," she said, hitting him again with the switch. "We're not even close to done yet." But it had no effect. When she jerked the reins to the side, Shy Guy threw his head up, clocking her right in the chin.

"Oooh," Izzy said, wincing but smiling a little. "That looks like it hurt."

Elena, startled, put a hand to her damaged face. Her shoulders trembled. Then she climbed off Shy

Guy's back, grabbed the reins, and hit him.

He tossed his head to the side, trying to get away, but she held the reins fast—and Shy Guy was too gentle to try to hurt her in his effort to escape.

He was a prisoner.

Rage filled Hanna to the brim. "Hey!" she shouted. Izzy grabbed her by the arm, but Hanna was already crawling over the old Chevy toward the fence. Shy Guy's ears perked forward. "HEY!"

Elena looked up, eyes wide, thinking she'd been caught. But when she saw Hanna and Izzy, the fear evaporated.

"Why, hello," she said, holding Shy Guy back when he tried to walk toward the fence to greet Hanna. He tossed his head again, but she tugged the reins down. "You really did a number on my horse. He refuses to collect on his canter."

"You messed up your own horse," said Hanna.

"He'd probably listen to you if you didn't hit him all the time," said Izzy.

Elena's face reddened. "The problem is you, not me. Bad behavior warrants punishment. It worked for my mom, and it works for me. He wouldn't be acting this way if you hadn't gotten your delinquent paws all over him. "

"We're not delinquents," snapped Izzy. Now she was mad.

"Oh, aren't you?" said Elena as she got back on Shy Guy. "Then how did you end up at a place like Quartz Creek Ranch?"

"You . . . you . . . !" Izzy probably would have climbed over the fence if it weren't for the barbed wire.

"Now, thanks to your distraction, he gets no dinner tonight," said Elena.

"That's messed up," said Hanna. "Not feeding him won't make him respond to you better."

"Bad behavior," Elena repeated, "warrants punishment."

Hanna's eyes turned blurry as angry tears started squeezing out of the corners of her eyes. "Give him back!" she cried. "You didn't even want him. You abandoned him."

Elena nudged Shy Guy with her knee and obediently, he turned around. "A temporary flaw in judgment," she said. "But a mistake is a mistake. Everyone makes them."

"You're the worst," said Hanna.

"Another thing you have wrong," she said. "With Star Dancer's help, I'm going to qualify for the Grand

Prix this year. Because I am, in fact, the best." She glanced up at the sky. "And unlike my mother, when I get to the Olympics, I'm not going to mess up on the piaffe. I'm going to bring home the gold."

"Fat chance," said Izzy. "You haven't been an Olympic hopeful in five years."

Elena huffed. "How dare you. I really ought to press charges against those Bridles for how you horrible kids kidnapped Star Dancer." She clicked to Shy Guy and nudged him with her heels, and reluctantly he started walking away. "But it's not worth my time."

Hanna and Izzy stood, speechless, as Elena rode off. Shy Guy twisted his neck around to look back at Hanna, but Elena yanked his head back again. Soon he was nothing more than a vague gray shape disappearing into the trees.

When he was gone, Hanna broke down.

"She can't do that!"

"I think she just did," said Izzy.

Hanna furiously wiped her face with her arm as they walked back to meet Paul. They found the ranch manager ogling a new pair of Wranglers. He dropped the jeans when he saw the tears running down Hanna's face.

"What happened?" he asked.

"Elena Baxter," she said, sniffling.

Paul took off his hat and pressed it to his chest. "You should stay away from that woman," he said. "She's disturbed."

"Evil is more like it," said Izzy.

He shook his head. "I talked to a few folks in town after she took Shy Guy," he said, nodding at the feed store owner. "Her mother, Juliet Baxter? As an old lady, she was no walk in the park either—an even worse woman than her daughter, or so Mark told me. Real hard on her animals and real hard on her family. Elena Baxter maybe hasn't had the easiest life."

"So what?" demanded Hanna between hiccups. "That's no excuse for what she's doing to Shy Guy."

"Not saying it is," agreed Paul. "But I wouldn't doubt that the late Mrs. Baxter treated Elena much the way Elena treats her horses."

In the back of the truck on the way home, as Paul blared country music from the stereo and the girls ate their ice cream, Izzy leaned over.

"At least we know where she lives now," she said, just quiet enough that Paul couldn't hear. Hanna's eyes widened. She was about to say something when, in the front seat, Paul turned the music down.

"How's the ice cream, ladies?" he called back to them.

"Hooo grrd!" replied Izzy, her mouth suddenly full of ice cream. How she'd done that, Hanna couldn't guess.

Paul laughed at Izzy's answer. "Okay, I'll take that as an *excellent*."

So Izzy was pretty sneaky too? Hanna filed that information away for later.

CHAPTER TWENTY-ONE

After dinner that night, when Madison left them alone to go for her biweekly swim, Izzy and Hanna filled in Rae Ann on what they'd seen near the feed store that day.

"Poor Shy Guy!" she said, covering her mouth. "That woman's so horrible. You have to tell Ma Etty what you saw."

"And then what?" said Izzy. "Ma Etty already tried everything she could."

"Elena Baxter is smart. Too smart." Hanna flopped on her bunk bed, arms spread-eagle to keep the heat off her sides. "We have to outsmart her."

"How?" asked Rae Ann. She crossed her legs on

her bed and stared down at her toes. "I can't out-smart anyone, even my folks—and they usually have their noses buried in Bibles. The only thing I can do is sound like someone's mom on the phone. Need me to pretend to be anyone?"

No one had an answer to that. Izzy suddenly sat up.

"I think we need some fresh ideas. We're spinning our wheels in here. Why don't we ask the guys?"

"It's late," said Rae Ann.

"So? Let's say we're bored with Madison gone and challenge them to a game of dice. Fletch won't care. Josh says he's always in his room reading anyway."

Hanna agreed, and the three of them got up and left the girls' bunkhouse. They knocked on the door to the boys' cabin, and Cade answered.

"Whoa, hey. What's up?"

"Hey. We're, uh, bored. And thought you guys might want to play dice."

Fletch came out of his room, and sure enough, he was holding a book in his hand. He was in sweatpants and still had his cowboy hat on. It had partially slipped down over his face.

"Dice?" he said, peering out the door looking for Madison. "Oh, I guess Maddie went swimming.

Well, okay. Come on in. But only for half an hour, okay?"

"Okay," the kids agreed.

Fletch, yawning, went back into his room but left the door cracked. When they were all set up for dice on the little table, Josh lowered his head and narrowed his eyes at the three girls.

"What's really going on?" he whispered.

"We found out where Elena Baxter lives," Izzy whispered back. Cade and Josh exchanged a surprised look.

"How?"

"We saw her near the feed store today," said Hanna. "She was abusing Shy Guy again."

"No!" Cade bared his teeth. "So it's all true. And the Bridles let her take him?"

"What could they have done?" demanded Josh.

"Shh," said Rae Ann, glancing around fearfully. "Fletch."

"Right, sorry."

"That's why we need your help," said Izzy.

"How can we possibly help?" said Cade. "Don't get me wrong, I want to. But . . ."

"But nothing," interrupted Josh. "We'll help however we can."

"We need a plan," Hanna said. "We know where she lives. We know what she's doing. But how do we prove it?"

"The sheriff has to see it," said Josh, with total certainty. Everyone at the table turned to him. "What? Seriously. That's it. That's all you have to do."

"How do you suggest we do that?" said Rae Ann, voice dripping with sarcasm. Everyone looked surprised at that.

"I don't know, Little Debbie," said Josh, rising to her tone. "He needs to catch her in the act. Maybe we can get a recording of it, something you can show to him."

But before Josh could say anything else, Hanna glanced at Izzy knowingly.

The phone.

"No way," said Izzy. "If they find out I brought it . . ."

"So what?" said Hanna. "This is bigger than that."

Now the others looked confused. "Brought what?" asked Cade.

"Hanna . . ." Izzy trailed off, looking frightened for the first time. "That was our secret!"

But Hanna plowed on. "Izzy brought a phone to

camp," she said. "Sorry, Izzy." Rae Ann gasped, but the boys didn't look surprised.

"Big whoop," said Josh. "Cade snuck in an MP3 player." Then understanding dawned on him. "The camera in the phone!"

"Shh!" said Rae Ann again. She grabbed the dice and threw them just as Fletch opened the door to check on them.

Cade pretended to write down a score. Josh said, "Dang it! I should have cashed out while I was ahead."

When the door was closed again, Hanna leaned forward, feeling a rush now that they finally had an idea.

"So we sneak in," said Izzy, "and wait until we see what we're looking for, then film it?"

"Sneak in?" squeaked Rae Ann, sinking back in her chair as if the physical distance would keep her from getting involved—and getting in trouble.

Hanna agreed. "We can't. If we break the law, we're as bad as she is."

Izzy arched an eyebrow at her. "Oh, all about not breaking laws now?"

Josh and Cade watched them curiously.

"Yeah," said Hanna, narrowing her eyes. "I am. This is trespassing, Izzy. That's kind of a big deal."

"But if we can get video, Hanna—if we can prove that Elena is mistreating Shy Guy, it won't matter. We can sneak in and sneak out without her seeing us. I know we can." She shot Hanna a look. "And I know *you* definitely can."

Rae Ann covered her ears. "I can't believe I'm hearing this."

"Then stay out of it," snapped Izzy.

"Whoa, whoa," said Josh. "Okay now, take it easy. We're all in this together to save Shy Guy. At least we have a plan, even if it bends a few rules."

He was right. It would have to do.

"All right," said Hanna, shoring up her resolve. "Let's do it. But how?"

CHAPTER TWENTY-TWO

Over the next few days, the five of them put the finishing touches on their plan. Hanna was glad they'd brought in Josh and Cade, because it was easier to plug up the holes with everyone involved.

On the day they'd picked, they waited until after lunchtime to put their plan in motion.

"Free time starts at two today," Madison told them over lunch. "Everyone know what they want to do?"

Izzy's hand shot in the air. "Free ride," she said.

"Me too," chimed in Hanna.

Madison looked surprised. "Okay, sure," she said. "I can work with you two."

"Actually," said Rae Ann, "Madison, I was hoping we could go swimming this afternoon and you could show me some things. I know you're really good at it, and I was thinking I'd join my school's swim team next year."

Madison's eyes lit up. "Well, yeah! Of course, Rae Ann. Ma Etty will need to coordinate getting you a temporary gym pass, but . . ."

"Not a problem," said Ma Etty, putting a fresh bowl of salad on the table. "Rae Ann expressed interest the other day, so I made sure we had some."

"Ma Etty," piped up Cade, "are you still planning to pick up baby chicks this afternoon?"

She glanced up. "Yes, I think so. Paul already set up a spot for them in the cattle barn."

"Can I go with you during free time? They're so cute. I want to help pick them out."

"I don't see why not," she said, then glanced at Fletch. "Weren't you and Josh going to go help Paul brand some new cattle? No one will be around to watch Hanna and Izzy."

"That's still the plan," said Fletch. "Since Josh says he wants to get into cattle ranching someday."

Mr. Bridle, who'd kept quiet until now, shrugged. "I think Izzy and Hanna will be fine, as long as they stay in the arena. They've both become excellent horsewomen. And I'll be in the house doing paperwork anyway, if something comes up." He smiled at both of them, and Hanna felt a pang of guilt. But it was quickly swept away by the memory of Elena working Shy Guy to the bone.

"All right then," said Madison. "It's settled."

And the plan was under way.

\\\\\\\\\\\\\\\\\\\\\\\\\\\\\\\\\\\\\\

Once Fettucini and Lacey were tacked up, Hanna and Izzy made a point of making a few circuits around the arena. Madison and Rae Ann left for the pool, and Ma Etty and Cade drove off in her truck. When they were alone, Hanna took Lacey back inside and put her away. They'd already doubled once, and hiding one horse was easier than hiding two.

"Plus," Hanna said, "Fettucini's a faster getaway vehicle."

Izzy beamed proudly at that.

They pulled out the copy of the town map they'd drawn, based off the one tacked up in the barn, and Hanna opened the arena gate.

The hardest part would be getting all the way down Bridlemile Road, down to the spot where the trail diverged from the road, without anyone seeing them. They decided to walk Fettucini instead of riding him, to appear less conspicuous if Mr. Bridle happened to glance out the window.

According to the map, the trail split before it joined Main Street, its upper fork curving northeast behind the feed store lot. They weren't sure of the exact location of Elena's property, but it would get them close enough.

Hopefully.

They took the north fork and encountered no one besides a farmer driving his tractor through a field. Soon the skeletal remains of cars and tractors appeared to their right, behind a barbed wire fence.

At the edge of the feed store lot's scrapyard, a new fence started that had to be Elena's. Hanna's stomach turned over. It was a lot to hope that Elena Baxter would be on the same schedule today as before, but hope was all they had. There was a spot in the fence that had been broken and recently, it looked like, repaired.

"We should get off here," Hanna said as they rounded a grove of trees on their left. To their right was the open field where they'd seen Elena and Shy Guy riding.

Izzy and Hanna dismounted, and Izzy led Fettucini into the trees, where she tied him to a hefty branch. When she reappeared, she brandished her camera phone.

"Ready?" she asked.

"Ready," said Hanna.

She put on a pair of thick leather gloves she'd slipped off a hook in the tack room and held the barbed wire fence open so Izzy could slip through. Hanna passed the gloves between the wires and Izzy did the same for her.

Her heart beat faster. The bushes hid them for now, but if Elena was close by, she'd see them for sure.

Once both girls emerged safely on the other side, they snuck around the pasture's perimeter, pushing through the low brush. Up ahead, the ground sloped up to a corral, a small white barn, and a beige farmhouse.

"Let's take the back fence," said Izzy, pointing to the far north side of the pasture, which was lined with greenery. "We can at least stick to the trees and bushes there."

It was slow going. Bushes with thorns snagged

their jeans as they went, and they still hadn't spotted Elena or Shy Guy yet.

Then they heard a door creak, and Hanna pulled Izzy behind a small tree. Up ahead of them, the barn door opened, and Elena led out Shy Guy. He was covered in dirt and mud, and his head hung low. Hanna's heart reached out to him, but they had to stay hidden.

Elena walked Shy Guy away from Hanna and Izzy's hiding spot, over to the corral, where she attached a long longe line to his halter. She began shouting commands at him and held out the whip. Seeing it, Shy Guy's eyes widened, and he jumped into a trot.

"Ugh, that's all wrong," Elena said, stopping him. She batted his ears with her hand, and he yanked his head away. *No wonder he'd been head shy*, thought Hanna, fury boiling up inside her.

Elena tossed out the longe line again and shook it. "Come on now," she called, smacking Shy Guy with the whip so hard the noise echoed. "Trot!"

At the command, Shy Guy leapt immediately into a trot, his eyes bulging with fear that he'd done it wrong.

"Get out the phone," whispered Hanna. Izzy

fumbled for it, and it almost fell to the ground. She saved it mid-air. But when she turned on the video camera, she let out a little moan.

"We're too far away for a decent video!"

Hanna ducked under the tree, and when Elena's back was turned, she jogged across the open expanse of field to the next tree, closer to the barn, upwind of the corral. On Shy Guy's next circuit, Izzy did the same. They kept moving this way until they were close enough that they could dash across to the barn itself and get a close-up view of the corral.

"Behind the barn," hissed Hanna, pointing.

"Check!" whispered Izzy.

The next time Elena was facing away from them, they sprinted across the largest expanse of field and ducked behind the side of the barn as she started coming back around.

They were still a good twenty yards off but close enough to get a decent shot.

"There. Got it," Izzy said, holding up the phone and pressing the button to record.

Watching Elena's cruelty unfold without being able to say or do anything made Hanna's body shake. She stood, covering her mouth, as Elena hit Shy Guy.

When Elena hit him the third time, a sob escaped Hanna's throat.

Elena spun and spotted them.

"You!" She threw the whip down, and Hanna knew only one thing—the same thing she'd known the few times store clerks and shopkeepers caught her stealing.

It was time to get out of there.

"Run!" Hanna yelled.

In her panic Izzy dropped the phone, and Hanna scrambled to pick it up. Izzy was already sprinting back the way they'd come when Hanna looked up again. Now outside of the corral, Elena was dashing after Izzy.

But Izzy's short legs couldn't stay ahead. Elena caught up in no time and seized Izzy by the arm.

"No!" cried Hanna. "Izzy!" But she also knew the top priority was getting the video footage to safety. Turning, she dashed the opposite direction from Elena Baxter: into the open barn door. Once inside, she slammed it closed behind her. That would buy her a few extra seconds.

Inside, the barn was dark, but the smell of horse manure overpowering. Hanna gagged.

This was where Elena Baxter was keeping Shy Guy.

Three stalls lined the right wall, and knowing she didn't have much time, Hanna peered in the first one. This was where she kept Shy Guy, she could tell—there was manure piled almost a foot high. Taking out the phone, which was still recording, she surveyed the catastrophe. She recorded mound after mound of manure and old, rotting hay.

Hanna thought maybe it had been true about Elena blowing the last of her money on Shy Guy. When she was rich, she paid someone to do her dirty work for her—but now there was no one.

Behind her, the door Hanna had come through banged opened.

There stood Elena, silhouetted by the afternoon sun, a howling Izzy clutched in one of her strong hands.

Hanna threw open the opposite door.

"Stop!" Elena screeched, but Hanna dashed out and sprinted as fast as her long, gangly legs could carry her, the phone still clutched in her hand.

CHAPTER TWENTY-THREE

Elena hadn't bothered chasing Hanna, with Izzy already her captive. But that didn't stop Hanna from running as fast as she could, back the way they'd snuck in, frightened, angry tears streaming down her face.

She squeezed through the fence, tearing her shirt on the barbed wire, but she didn't care. Back where Fettucini was still tied up, Hanna threw his reins over his neck and climbed on his back. He was harder to control than Lacey, but Hanna trusted him to get her home safe.

And he did, galloping home to Quartz Creek Ranch like the wind.

"Mr. Bridle!" Hanna shouted as she and Fettucini cantered up Bridlemile Road, passing the ranch house. "Ma Etty! Fletch! Madison!"

Ma Etty and Cade were climbing out of the truck when Hanna raced up to them.

"Whoa," said Ma Etty, holding up her hands. "What's going on? What are you doing riding out here? And why are you on Fettucini?"

"Can't explain," said Hanna, panting. She jumped off and handed Fettucini's reins to Cade. "It's Izzy. Elena Baxter has Izzy." Fumbling in her pocket, she took out the phone.

"What on earth is that?" asked Ma Etty as the ranch house's front door banged open.

"Who's callin' my name?" said Mr. Bridle. He took in the scene cautiously. "Someone going to explain to me what that horse is doing all lathered up?"

Hanna held out the phone, the video queued up. "Just watch," she said.

Ma Etty and Mr. Bridle peered at the screen. In tinny low-fi, Hanna could hear Elena shouting. Ma Etty covered her mouth, and a deep crease appeared in Mr. Bridle's brow.

"Elena has Izzy," Hanna said again, trying to impress upon them the urgent nature of their predicament. "She caught us filming her. We have to go help Izzy!"

Ma Etty and Mr. Bridle exchanged a long look. Then, without any words passing between them, Mr. Bridle nodded.

"Cade, go find Fletch. Tell him what's going on." He looked at Hanna. "Get in the truck. We're going to get our girl back—and our horse too."

\\

Hanna directed them to Elena's property, but this time, instead of taking the back way, the Bridles roared up the front drive. Up ahead, blue and red lights flashed—it was the sheriff, and as they pulled into the driveway, Hanna saw him putting tiny Izzy in the back of his car. Elena stood behind him with her arms crossed over her chest.

"Let her go!" Shouting, Hanna jumped out of the truck before it was completely stopped and raced toward the sheriff's car. "She didn't do anything wrong."

When the truck was parked, the Bridles hustled out after her. Right as he was about to slam the patrol car door, the sheriff looked up and his mouth dropped open.

"Mr. and Mrs. Bridle," he said, giving them each a nod. "I was about to call you. This girl's one of yours?" Izzy's head poked out of the door, and Hanna's chest twisted at the terrified look in her usually confident eyes.

"Of course she is," said Ma Etty, walking up to the car and helping Izzy out of it. The sheriff stepped back, clearly knowing better than to get between Ma Etty and one of her ranch kids.

"Hey," snapped Elena. "I'm pressing charges against that girl for trespassing."

Ma Etty glared at the other woman. "Sheriff Handy, you're arresting the wrong person." She pointed directly at Elena. "That woman neglects and abuses her horses."

"That's quite an accusation, Etty," the sheriff said, glancing between them.

"I have proof," said Hanna, pulling the phone out. "She hits Shy Guy. I've seen her do it twice now, but this time I recorded it." She pressed PLAY on the video and passed it to the sheriff. "And she punishes him by withholding food."

"Those hooligans were trespassing on my

property," said Elena, trying to grab the phone away.

The sheriff held up a hand. "Let me watch," he warned her.

As the video played, his eyebrows drew together and his mouth slowly parted. When it was over, he stared long and hard at Elena, who no longer looked quite so certain that things would work out her way.

"This is truly atrocious, Ms. Baxter," he said, giving the phone back to Ma Etty. He not-so-subtly patted his badge. "Show me the barn, please."

"You can't use that as evidence," Elena said, growing frantic. "They were the ones who broke the law."

"I won't ask again, Ms. Baxter. Show. Me. The barn."

Hanna, Izzy, and the Bridles waited as Sheriff Handy looked inside the barn. When he returned, his face was ashen.

"It's obvious to me what's going on here," he said, taking off his hat. He rubbed his face. "And it is in my authority as county sheriff to reclaim and foster abused animals. But we both know I don't have the kind of room or resources for that. Etty, could you foster Ms. Baxter's horse for me?"

Hanna couldn't believe her ears. She and Izzy turned to each other and hugged.

"You can't give away my horse," roared Elena. "He's mine! I bought and paid for him! He's taking me to the Olympics!"

"Keep it down," snapped the sheriff, turning to her. "You better watch it, Ms. Baxter. The only reason I haven't thrown you into the back of my car is I think you're quite sick. But give me a reason to, and I'm happy to do it. And we all know that Olympics story is a crock—you've been telling everyone that for years."

"I'm calling my lawyer." Elena pulled out her phone and began dialing, but Sheriff Handy looked unconcerned.

"We'll let the lawyers work out the details," he said with a shrug.

The Bridles both nodded. "Of course," said Ma Etty gratefully. "Of course we'll take in the horse, Doug."

"Then go get your Shy Guy," he said to Hanna and Izzy. "Go take that poor horse home."

Elena was yelling angrily into her phone as Hanna walked to the corral where Shy Guy was standing, still attached to the longe line. Izzy opened the corral gate and waited outside while Hanna stepped in.

Shy Guy looked startled when she approached, and for a moment, she wondered if he was lost again—if everything they'd done together was washed away by Elena Baxter. But then his nostrils flared, and his ears pointed toward her. He took a step and then two in her direction, and she matched them, until her arms wrapped around his neck and his head curled over her shoulder.

"Good boy," she said, leaning her cheek against his soft throat, running her hands through his mane. "Oh, you good boy. I'm so sorry. No one's going to hurt you again. Not ever."

He let out a long sigh, as if he understood.

\\

Elena's squat husband came home while they waited for Paul to arrive with the trailer. Hanna led Shy Guy past where they stood by the police cruiser, answering Sheriff Handy's questions.

"How?" Elena demanded, startling girl and horse. "I don't get it. How did a talentless kid like you fix him? How did you get him to perform?"

Hanna blinked at her.

"I only loved him," she said. "I love him just the way he is."

Elena had no response. Her husband sighed.

"I hope you can understand," he said, putting an arm around Elena's shoulders. Hanna was surprised to see tears in Elena's eyes. "My wife has always tried so hard. But it was never enough, you know."

"Actually," Hanna said, "I do understand."

Soon the trailer came up the drive, and Paul parked the truck and let the ramp down. When Hanna led Shy Guy toward it, he jerked his head back, straining against the lead rope, eyes wide.

Hanna knew what he was remembering: the rain pelting the ground, Elena Baxter shouting and whipping him as she forced him into the trailer.

"Can I just ride him back?" Hanna asked.

Paul grinned and rubbed his hands together. "Just so happens I brought a saddle just in case."

"Perfect."

Hanna led Shy Guy away from the trailer and ran her hand down his neck for a long time.

He was fearful, but not lost the way he used to be. She still recognized Shy Guy in there, and Shy Guy still recognized her. Hanna knew they had some ground to make up.

Once he was calm again, Hanna saddled him and mounted. Izzy rode shotgun in the truck as she and Paul followed Hanna and Shy Guy home.

The sun was setting as they passed under the sign reading QUARTZ CREEK RANCH. Everyone had gathered out front of the ranch house, and a cheer went up as they walked up Bridlemile Road. Shy Guy hesitated at first, but with Hanna stroking his neck, he was convinced to approach the crowd.

After she got off and hugs were exchanged with everyone, Hanna led Shy Guy back to the barn. He had to smell it first to know it was their barn—the good barn—before he'd go in.

Inside, she slowly took off his bridle and saddle, and spent almost an hour cleaning him up. When she was done, she led him back to the stall with the nameplate reading "Shy Guy" and gave him two flakes of hay and a full bucket of grain.

CHAPTER TWENTY-FOUR

The last week at Quartz Creek Ranch was surprisingly somber. They would all have to leave soon—to go home and return to their regularly scheduled lives.

But it was especially so for Hanna. Every day she got to spend with Shy Guy was more valuable than diamonds. The kids and their trainers went on a trail ride together, and Shy Guy relished the climb up into the hills behind the ranch. They even had an impromptu race around the little lake they found in a secluded valley.

Shy Guy and Fettucini finished neck and neck. They weren't really sure who won.

Hanna was grateful to find Elena hadn't undone

all the ground she'd gained with Shy Guy. They fell back into their old pattern, and soon he even started letting Madison work with him. He didn't even seem to mind other people, as long as they kept their hands where he could see them.

As the final day approached, the idea of leaving Izzy and Rae Ann and Madison and everyone twisted Hanna's heart. She didn't know when she'd come to care about them all so much.

"There are always airplanes," Izzy said one night after lights-out, when Rae Ann was already asleep. They'd snuck out of the cabin and were sitting on the front stairs, talking in hushed voices. "You could come visit me in Phoenix. Or I could visit you in Michigan. And we could go see the Lawnchairs together!"

"Yes!" But Hanna knew it was unlikely either of their parents would foot the bill for a plane ticket. "They play Sturgis a lot. Home turf and everything."

They both knew this was probably good-bye, but they didn't say it. Popping in the earbuds, one each, they played the album all the way through one last time.

On the last day of camp, there were no chores and the kids were given free time to do whatever they wished around the ranch. Most of them chose riding, but Josh wanted to play bean bag toss with Paul. Hanna went and played with him during lunch and won four games in a row.

"Dang it, Hanna," he said in his lilting southern drawl. "When did you become so good at this game?"

"When you made me play it every day," she said, and he gave her one of his rare, lopsided smiles. She kind of hoped she'd see Josh again too.

At dinner that evening, Rae Ann started the waterworks when Ma Etty mentioned it was the last night, and Cade made sure everyone knew his e-mail address. Then they went back to their cabins and packed up their things. While Hanna was shoving clothes haphazardly into her duffel bag, a knock came at the door.

Madison opened it, and Ma Etty stepped inside.

"Hanna?" she asked. "Can we talk outside?"

Hanna nodded and followed her out onto the porch, and the door closed behind them.

"I called your mom." Hanna's stomach soured. Her mom? Had she done something wrong?

"Why?" asked Hanna.

"Because I wanted to tell her what a privilege it's been having you here at the ranch this summer. I explained a little about Shy Guy and how brave you were, and I suggested that if she could, she should come pick you up in person."

"In . . . person?" Her mom, here at the ranch? Hanna wanted to see her mom even less than she wanted to leave.

"She's flying in tomorrow. I thought I'd give you a heads-up. She's looking forward to seeing you."

Hanna's head drooped. Ma Etty put a hand on her shoulder.

"I know you and your mom have had a rocky relationship. But I think it's important she see how much you've grown here and what a great thing you've done working with Shy Guy."

"I don't know . . ."

"Trust me, Hanna. She's your mom. She loves you, and I know she wants to understand you. I think that seeing what you've done here will help."

She nodded. There wasn't anything she could do about it now. "Okay."

"Don't worry," said Ma Etty, smiling. "It will be fine. I promise."

\\\\\\\\\\\\\\\\\\\\\\\\\\\\\\\\\\\\\\

The next morning, while the other kids loaded their things into the old Econoline van to head to the airport, Hanna saddled up Shy Guy and did a few exercises with him in the arena. Izzy appeared outside the fence and leaned against it.

"Looking good, killer," she said. "You guys are awesome together."

Hanna and Shy Guy sidled over, and Hanna dismounted. Izzy slipped through the bars and, without a preamble, wrapped her up in a hug. "Don't you forget about me."

Hanna laughed, thinking about spiders crawling around in her bed. "It would be impossible to forget you."

"Your mom's here." With that, Izzy affectionately punched Hanna's shoulder, turned, and climbed back out. Then she was gone, and Hanna blinked back tears.

Sure enough, her mom walked around the side of the barn and paused when she saw Hanna. She didn't say anything as Hanna led Shy Guy over and opened the gate to the arena. Her mom cautiously stepped through, her shoes already muddy from walking around.

"Hi," said Hanna.

Her mom smiled a cautious smile, but her eyes were happier and brighter than she'd ever seen them.

"Oh, my Hanna." Her mom leaned forward and

put her arms around her. She kissed the top of Hanna's head, then stepped back to observe Shy Guy. "Wow. He's so gorgeous. Like one of your toy horses."

"Yeah," said Hanna. "I thought the same thing." Slowly her mom reached out one hand toward Shy Guy, who, surprisingly, didn't flinch away. She petted his soft nose, and Shy Guy blew out a gust of air.

"Tell me everything," her mom said. "Everything. Please."

\\

When Hanna was done, her mom was crying. She hugged Hanna again and held onto her tightly. Hanna felt tears land on her hair.

"You're incredible," her mom said. "You're such an incredible girl. Ma Etty told me how proud she is of you. How frightened you were and how hard you worked anyway. It's all thanks to this guy?"

Hanna nodded. Her mom released her, and Hanna patted Shy Guy's strong neck. He dipped his head as if to say, *Yes, that's me.*

"I guess," said Hanna. "He's the one who's incredible. You wouldn't believe the things he knows, Mom. He's smart. He's sweet. He's kind."

"Sounds like a girl I know," her mom said.

"And he's so eager to please. But to Elena . . . it was never enough." Hanna paused, choosing her words carefully. "I know how that feels, you know. For nothing you do to be enough."

Her mom sucked in a breath, then gave a slow nod.

"Hanna," she said, voice shaking a little, "I . . . I think we have some things to talk about."

"I think so too."

"The stealing. It has to stop."

"I know." Hanna swallowed back tears. "I didn't do it because I like it, Mom. I did it because I . . . I was so angry at you. Because I tried my hardest to be the best, to be the daughter you wanted, and you kept telling me it wasn't enough. That I wasn't good enough for you. So I thought stealing would show you how good I'd been. That I could also be an awful daughter, if I wanted."

"Oh, Hanna." Her mom's eyes turned glossy. "I'm so sorry. I'm sorry I ever made you feel that way. You are exactly the daughter I want. More than! You're perfect." She stroked Shy Guy again, and he leaned into her hand. His brown eyes observed them both with a gentle kindness.

"If I promise to be better," her mom began, snif- fling, "will you promise not to steal anymore?"

"Of course!" Hanna felt something inside her break. "Of course, Mom."

This time, her mother's embrace was a bear hug. When she was finished, her mom let her go and said, "And what about Shy Guy, here? You must be so sad to be leaving him behind. After what you told me, I'm sure he'll be sad to see you go. You know, there are some horse barns near our house. Maybe we could ask Ma Etty if we could take him with us?"

Hanna's heart nearly exploded out of her chest. Keep Shy Guy? Oh, how she wanted to! Shy Guy understood her in a way only Shy Guy could, the same way she understood him.

But she shook her head.

"I can't," she said quietly. "I can't ever ask him to get into a trailer again—not after what Elena did to him."

Her mother's eyes shone with unshed tears. She wiped them and nodded.

"I understand," she said. "You are so brave." Summoning a smile, she added, "Now show me what you two can do! I hear good things."

Taking a deep breath, Hanna stuck her foot in

the stirrup and pushed herself up. Once she was on Shy Guy's back, everything was perfect.

As they walked along the fence, Hanna let out just enough rein for him to glide into a trot, and then more rein until they fell into a sweet, smooth extended trot.

Then they were sailing—no, *flying*—together around the arena. Shy Guy's powerful hooves pounded the dirt, and his shoulders rippled, all silver muscle and shine. And the wind had never felt better as it raced through Hanna's hair.

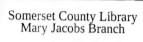
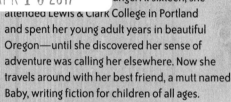

...rew up riding horses ...ange. At sixteen, she attended Lewis & Clark College in Portland and spent her young adult years in beautiful Oregon—until she discovered her sense of adventure was calling her elsewhere. Now she travels around with her best friend, a mutt named Baby, writing fiction for children of all ages.

AMBER J. KEYSER is happiest when she is in the wilderness with her family. Lucky for her, the rivers and forests of Central Oregon let her paddle, hike, ski, and ride horses right outside her front door. When she isn't adventuring, Amber writes fiction and nonfiction for young readers and goes running with her dog, Gilda.

ACKNOWLEDGMENTS

We have to thank our superhero agent, Fiona Kenshole, for suggesting that we write this series in the first place, for encouraging us to work together, and for championing us all the way to publication. Huge thanks to Anna and our wonderful team at Darby Creek for bringing Quartz Creek Ranch to life. Thank you to Heidi Siegel for all her horsey expertise; to Cesca for letting us use her band name; and to Whitney for dropping everything to make sure this book became a reality.

We also want to remember Spring, the wonderful gray horse who serves as the real-life inspiration behind Shy Guy. When Kiersi was a young girl, she was entrusted with rehabilitating an abandoned horse named Spring—from foundered to healthy, from forgotten to loved. You went through so much, and were still so full of heart.

Wherever you are, Spring, this one's for you.